The carriage was
Cheltenham. Ano
they would be the
mouth to commen
before she could say a word, there was the sound of a shot being fired, and the shouted command to 'Stand!'. Isabella screamed, the door was thrown open, and Anne found herself confronted by the barrel of a pistol.

So soon as Isabella could be induced to stop screaming, the heavily masked gentleman who had appeared in the doorway lowered his pistol, and announced in civilized tones, "I have no quarrel with members of your sex. I beg your pardon for the interruption, and if you have no objections to make, shall be on my way."

Anne said gravely that they had not the least objection in the world. "Then I will bid you God speed. Ladies—your servant."

With that, he was gone, and their carriage jerked into motion.

"Well!" said Anne, "There is an extraordinary adventure to befall us! Whatever is one to make of *that,* do you suppose?"

Also by Sarah McCulloch

A LADY FOR LUDOVIC
A MOST INSISTENT LADY
NOT QUITE A LADY
MERELY A GENTLEMAN

and published by Corgi Books

A Perfect Gentleman

Sarah McCulloch

CORGI BOOKS

A DIVISION OF TRANSWORLD PUBLISHERS LTD

A PERFECT GENTLEMAN

A CORGI BOOK 0 552 12049 9

First publication in Great Britain

PRINTING HISTORY
Corgi edition published 1982

This book is set in Fairfield 10 on 11 pt.

Corgi Books are published by Transworld Publishers Ltd.,
Century House, 61–63 Uxbridge Road, Ealing, London W5 5SA

Made and printed in the United States of America by
Offset Paperbacks, Dallas, Pennsylvania.

A Perfect Gentleman

CHAPTER ONE

Anne Fredericks had reached the age of very nearly four and twenty without her hand ever once having been solicited in marriage nor herself ever having been the possessor of a single accredited lover; which peculiar and unhappy circumstance could be ascribed, however, neither to any disagreeableness in her person nor to any lack of amiability in her temper.

At the time of writing she was in the full bloom of her beauty. Her figure, though slight, was elegant; her hair, of a soft and almost silvery tone, curled very prettily without any need of being artifically frizzled nor put up in papers, whilst her face was a perfect oval, with regular features and a nose which had achieved just sufficient in length to be spared the ignominy of being dubbed retroussé. Her colour was not high—indeed, she inclined rather to paleness and would not have recourse to the rouge pot no matter how her sister-in-law might beg—but her eyes were fine and sparkling, of that shade which can best be described as blue-grey, and the firmly delineated line of a small but determined jaw saved her from any hint of insipidity.

In character she was quiet, and somewhat retiring, never pushing herself forward where there was the least hint that she might not be wanted, yet always ready, when applied to, to give a forthright and common-sensical opinion or offer what had come to be relied upon as very sound advice. She had, besides, a strong sense of the ridiculous, which allowed her upon occasion to see humour where others might not perhaps have remarked it, and in general successfully managed to combine gentleness of disposition with a firm adherence to principle and a dislike of all that was sham. Her greatest fault might have been said to be her persistent undervaluing of her own worth. She was harder upon herself than upon anyone else, never seeing weaknesses in *them* but what she could find corresponding ones in her own person. If she could only have learnt to be a little more assertive in her own behalf, she might not now have reached the advanced age of (almost) four and twenty and still remain Anne Fredericks.

She lived, and had done these past several years, with her brother and sister-in-law, in the small village of Boswood, some few miles out of Oxford, where the chiefest of her occupations was the tending of her own small patch of garden and playing with Isabella's infant sons, George and Henry, two lusty young men of six and five years of age respectively, who, unlike their aunt, never shrank from putting themselves forward wherever and whenever the opportunity presented itself; whilst the chiefest of her social amusements consisted of her once-monthly drive into Oxford with Isabella, to gaze at the shops and seek to glean some idea of what the latest fashions might be, and her once-a-week visit to her old governess, Miss Morcomb, now running a select girls' seminary in Abingdon.

It was not choice, but rather circumstance, which had led to her present cloistered existence. At the age of eighteen, Anne had had the great misfortune to lose both parents in a typhus epidemic. Shortly after their demise, she herself had fallen victim to the same disease; and already in a weakened state through the grief of her loss, and through the long hours of loving care with which she had tended her stricken parents, had been so gravely ill that for some while her own life had been despaired of. Adam had left his Isabella, then enceinte with her first born, and journeyed post-haste into Buckinghamshire to be with her. Devoted nursing by Miss Morcomb, and the constant presence of a beloved brother, had eventually pulled her through, but the doctors shook their heads and declared her constitution to have been permanently impaired; from henceforth she was to be regarded as fragile, and treated accordingly: watched over and guarded like a frail plant, carefully sheltered from all the bustle and buffetings of the outside world.

If Anne, for her part, had long since ceased to consider her constitution as being in the least degree inpaired, nor herself as being any more or less fragile than the next person, she nevertheless accepted—not quite meekly, but at any rate with resignation—the restrictions imposed upon her by an anxious brother. The fact was, that the death of both parents, at a time when he himself had been absent from the family home, followed by the so narrowly avoided loss of a sister, had had a more prolonged and damaging effect upon Adam than it had upon Anne. The impairment of her constitution had proved but temporary: the impairment of her brother's spirits, she was sadly inclined to believe, was like to prove permanent. Adam had ever been of a serious, not to say grave, disposition, but the seriousness had been enlivened by that same ready sense of the ridiculous, that same sly appreciation of the bizarre and the quirky, which both the Fredericks children had inherited from their father. Since the tragedy, all sense of the ridiculous had gone: the bizarre could only exasperate, the quirky only offend. Gravity alone remained, and with it a kind of nervous irritability which led him to impose not only upon his sister, but upon himself and his wife, a régime which came close to being that of a recluse. Adam Fredericks had lost two of the people who meant most to him in life and had never recovered from that loss: in six long years, he had never learnt to laugh again.

Anne had come, insensibly, to feel that to expect enjoyment *now* was to be almost guilty of a crime. To hanker after balls, and frivolity, and the company of other young folk, betrayed a callous lack of feeling, a preoccupation with self, which could only be deprecated. She submitted, therefore, with good grace, even if, at times, with aching heart, to an existence from which many of the normal pleasures of youth must be excluded.

The only occasion on which she ever danced was once a year, at Christmas, when the estate workers came up to the house to be wined and dined in the servants' hall, and Anne led off the dancing, afterwards, with Bailey, the steward. Angus Bailey, at two and thirty, was the youngest gentleman of her acquaintance, always excepting her own brother; but Angus was happily married with a full brood of little ones: *he* could hardly be seen as a figure of romance. Neither could John Martineau, their nearest neighbour, who occasionally stepped over to inquire whether there were any errands he might perform "for the ladies". Mr. Martineau was still two years off fifty, and not, as Isabella frequently observed, too old to make a husband; but as yet he had shown no inclination to take the plunge, and in any case (as Isabella, with a sigh, was also prone to point out) wore flannel waistcoats for fifty of the fifty-two weeks in the year and woollen mufflers for at least thirty.

It was neither flannel waistcoats nor woollen mufflers that would put Anne off—though, to be sure, they could scarcely be classed as desirable garments for a prospective husband to be wrapping himself in—but the fact that Mr Martineau, for all his well-meaning, and the not inconsiderable number of years which he had lived in the world, was almost totally devoid of either good sense or intelligent conversation. If a man who could sit half the evening by one's fireside with no more brilliant contribution to make to the general entertainment than the repeated observation of "its having been a fine year for cabbages, and I shall tell Joliffe to bring you over three heads in the morning, so I shall" was the best that she could hope for, then she preferred to remain single.

The vainglory of such a statement—"prefer" to remain single? What choice, pray, did she suppose that *she* had in the matter?—could not but bring a slight, rueful smile to her lips. John Martineau might proffer heads of cabbages, but had as yet shown no signs of making any proposal of marriage; and if John Martineau did not do so, then she was sure she did not know of anyone else who might. There was always Dr. Walsh, perhaps. He was not yet completely in his dotage—he could still get about quite well, given plenty of time and the assistance of a supporting arm—and at least he did not talk of cabbages. Or how about Mr Mallerby, the music master at Miss Morcomb's school? *He* was still a comparative stripling, and even if he did suffer rather horribly from moist palms there was nothing else particularly amiss with him; not that she knew of; and approaching middle age as she was, she could scarcely afford the luxury of being choosy.

With such wry philosophical reflections did Anne seek to console herself, and on the whole succeeded pretty well. She was not a person who wished to be discontented with life—she took no pleasure from bemoaning her lot or from railing against a cruel fate. She could find plenty to make her happy; and even if she could not be fulfilled she could always be useful.

It should not be supposed from the foregoing that Anne Fredericks was in any way deficient in the sphere of female emotion; on the contrary. There had been a romantic interlude even in her circumscribed existence: she had once met a young man at Cheltenham and had danced two dances with him—that was how she chose to think of it *now*, paring it down to the barest of bare bones and indulging in a little laugh at her own expense, which was perhaps something she was rather too much prone to do. The truth of the matter was, the young man in question had appropriated to himself the major place in her girlish fantasies for many months after the event and had by no means been expunged from memory even now, five years further on, when girlish fancies had been sternly abandoned in favour of what Miss Fredericks chose to designate a "more realistic approach to life". The name of Richard *still* caused her cheeks to glow with rather more vigour than was their wont: the sight of a well set up young man parading the streets of Oxford, or of Abingdon, or even of Boswood itself, and happening to possess hair of a particular shade of black— for that there *were* shades of black, she would be the first to testify— could still cause a momentary flutter before she took herself in hand. (Or before the young man turned round and revealed a face like a sheep or cheeks as plump and full as a plum pudding.)

It would be useless to pretend the episode was forgot: it was not; and frequently entered, unbidden, into her thoughts even now. Of all the towns in England, Cheltenham must be the one that held the fondest place in her heart. The claims of others might be superior in point of interest, or importance, or historical association, but Cheltenham was by far the most dear, hallowed as it was by the one hint of romance that had ever entered her life.

Such being the case, it may perhaps be imagined with what mixed emotions—apprehension—delight—incredulity—she greeted the news that she was to go *back* there.

'I have stipulated for a month,' said Isabella. 'And if I cannot succeed in wangling more out of him once we are actually there—'

'You never mean to say that you have prevailed upon *Adam* to come?'

'Oh! Not Adam. He is grown into such a stay-at-home it would be pointless even to suggest it. No, he is to remain here with Nurse and the children whilst you and I go gallivanting . . . so!' Isabella clapped her hands together and laughed, in triumph. 'What have you to say to that?'

'I scarcely know what to say! I am at a loss to imagine how you ever contrived.'

'Oh, I chose my moment . . . we married women have our ways and means, as I trust you shall very soon discover for yourself, for I make no pretence: I have arranged this trip for one reason and one reason only—you may guess what it is. I do not mind telling you that I was never more disgusted in my life than when John Martineau failed to come up to scratch the other night. I had it quite settled in my mind that he would do so—you will have remarked the cunning way I drew Adam out of the room for ten minutes? *Expressly* to give him the chance of declaring himself?'

'Yes,' said Anne. 'That is when he made me the offer of three head of cabbages.'

'Cabbages! Can the wretched fellow converse on no other subject?'

'If I am to be honest, I had just as soon he did not, for had he made me the offer of anything else I fear I should have been forced to decline; and that, you know, could hardly fail of being hurtful to his feelings.'

'*His* feelings? And what of yours? Whether you would have accepted or not is beside the point! That a man of very nearly fifty years of age, totally unattached, can sit here week after week, month after month, talking of cabbages and never once feeling the urge to start talking instead of *matrimony*—'

Anne, smiling, shook her head.

'I assure you I would much rather he did not . . . I am perfectly content with the way things are.'

'Nonsense!' said Isabella. 'And even if *you* are, *I* am certainly not. You may consider yourself, if you should prefer it, as coming to Cheltenham in order to benefit *me*—unless, of course, you would rather we made it Bath? I am perfectly willing. I settled for Cheltenham only because it involves less travel, but if you feel that Bath should be more to your liking—'

'No!' A hint of colour entered Anne's cheek. 'If we are to go anywhere at all, then I am quite agreeable to its being Cheltenham.'

When once Isabella took an idea into her head, she lost no time in the promoting of it. Scarce three weeks after the scheme had first been mooted, it was being put into operation. They left for Cheltenham on a fine, clear Monday morning at the beginning of the season. Lodgings had been taken with a Mrs Gardner, near to the Royal Crescent. Isabella had wanted the High Street—'for it is always as well to be at the hub'—but Mrs Gardner's was where Anne had stayed before, and Adam could be satisfied that it was both clean and respectable.

'I should worry if you were in the High Street. There

is too much hustle and bustle—too many smart folk busy about their comings and goings. I shall feel more at ease if I know you are with Mrs Gardner. Mrs Gardner is a friend of Miss Morcomb.'

It was a recommendation that could not be denied: they had duly settled for Mrs Gardner and for Adam's peace of mind. He stood now on the front steps, along with little George and Henry, supervising their departure—directing the coachman to "take every care" and to "keep a close watch for any suspicious characters that may be met with along the way"—directing Isabella to "make sure Anne does not tire herself" and Anne to "run no risks with your health . . . I would not have you come back looking more fagged than when you went off."

She had not been aware that she *was* looking fagged—indeed, taking one final glance at herself before leaving her room, she had been complacently inclined to feel a degree of satisfaction. She had admittedly refused to spend money on a quite outrageously priced satin bonnet which had caught Isabella's eye on their last visit to Oxford—and which, with characteristic impetuosity, Isabella had urged her to buy—but to make up for that she had refurbished one of her old favourites with a length of jonquil ribbon and had been flattering herself that it became her rather well. Adam, it seemed, however, had other notions.

'Have you not been sleeping properly? It looks to me as though you have not.' He regarded her, searchingly, an anxious frown creasing his brow, which was already a great deal more creased than it should have been at the age of twenty-eight. He was very much alike to his sister in person, but with hair a shade darker and eyes inclining rather more towards grey than to blue. 'I hope the excitement is not proving too much for you. If it is, you must say so at once. It is not too late to cancel. Mrs Gardner will understand. There is no use setting out if you are tired before you even begin.'

'I am not in the least tired,' said Anne.

'Are you not? Are you quite certain? There is a something about you—'

She was at pains to reassure him. He was one who must

always be searching for signs of fatigue where she was concerned: she was accustomed to allow him the indulgence of his solicitude, even as she retained the right to be just as robust as she chose. It was Isabella who broke in, scoldingly, with: 'I wish you will not always be seeking to undermine our female vanity . . . here is Anne looking perfectly charming, and you doing your utmost to convince her she is nothing but a wreck.'

'Not at all. I implied no such thing. She is as pretty as ever—and so too are you! It is only—'

'Only nothing,' said Isabella. 'We have established that we are both of us as pretty as ever: you will do a great deal better to leave it at that.'

'Well! Very well. But you must send me word as soon as you arrive. I shall wish to know that you have got there safely.'

'Of course. You shall hear from us by every post.'

'I do not insist on *every* post, but at least the first. The roads can be treacherous—there is no knowing what hazards one may not encounter.'

'My dear Adam!' Isabella stooped, to kiss farewell to the children. 'You make it sound as though we were journeying to the Antipodes . . . we are only going to *Cheltenham!*'

CHAPTER TWO

Cheltenham . . . it was a name which could not but have a powerful effect upon the emotions. Impossible not to look back and to remember! Sternly though she might chide herself—for what, pray, was there to recall? One chance encounter with a young man called Richard, who had condescended to dance two dances with her and had very likely never given her a moment's thought ever since; still her mind would dwell upon it, do what she would to divert her attention elsewhere. The scenery, for instance, was very pretty—the day remarkably fine—Isabella was looking charmingly in a new pelisse of French green trimmed with gold braid, and once upon a time she had danced two dances with a young man called Richard . . .

If "two dances" were but the bare bones of it, and the way in which she characteristically sought to give herself a set down, it had on the other hand to be admitted that there was not such a *very* great deal more to flesh the story out. A nineteen-year old Anne had been recommended to try the waters as a means of putting the roses back into her cheeks (though roses had never been there in the first place: she had been pale from infancy) and Cheltenham had been fixed on as being not only the nearest of all the watering places but the one least calculated to agitate or over-excite. Adam, though already in the throes of that melancholy from which he was never completely to recover, had not at that stage been so nervous of his sister's welfare as he was later to become: he had readily agreed upon her going off, in the capable charge of Miss Morcomb, whilst he himself had remained at home, at Boswood, with Isabella, by that time pregnant once again and expecting Master Henry.

Miss Morcomb and Anne had taken lodgings with Miss Morcomb's friend from schooldays, Mrs Gardner. They had passed the major part of their time in strolling peaceably about the town, admiring the churches and gardens, and the displays in the shop windows. They had gone early each day to the Pump Room, and once or twice to the theatre. On several evenings they had attended at the Assembly Rooms, but although officially out of mourning Anne had not felt herself up to the demands of dancing. Her feet might long to be out there, jigging in time to the music, but her legs, she knew, were not yet strong enough to sustain her through the length of a whole set: she had been obliged merely to sit on the side and observe.

Wistfully—for what young woman of nineteen would not be wistful in such a situation?—she had watched the other dancers, noting with amusement, in spite of her wistfulness, the various flirtations which were conducting, noting which of the ladies were pleased with their partners and which were not, which gentlemen were bored and which striving to impress. One gentleman in particular had held her attention above all others. She had not known *then* that his name was Richard (it had ever been a favourite with her, right from the time of her having learnt in the schoolroom about the Lionheart) but he must in any case have stood out from the crowd, be his name romantic Richard or common or garden John or Henry. He was the sort of young man who might be depended upon to cause palpitations in the breast of any susceptible young female—and Anne, at the age of nineteen, had been every bit as susceptible as she ought to be. Six foot something or other of well-proportioned manhood, with a handsome face and an abundance of luxuriant black locks thrown in for good measure, was perfectly capable of rousing the most agreeable mixture of sensations within her. If she had not fallen in love *quite* upon the spot, she had certainly succumbed within the first ten minutes.

He had been there again the second night, wearing a striped silk coat and breeches, with a splended white silk waistcoat, and looking, if such were possible, even more handsome than he had on the previous occasion (which upon reflection was not only possible but virtually mandatory, since by now Anne was indulging girlish fancies to the full, so that it would have been a sad let down indeed if the young man had not greatly increased in his stock of personal beauty since last she had set eyes on him, which after all had been a good twenty-four hours since.)

Anne had watched him all evening, from her vantage point in the gallery. He had danced with only two young women, one of whom, even to Anne's anxious gaze, could only have been his sister—the facial resemblance was too marked to be denied—whilst the other had been so decidedly plain, albeit perfectly agreeable looking, that not the most humble of young women, always provided she had a reasonably pretty face and a trim figure, could have seen her in the light of a rival. The plain young woman, in any case, had seemed rather to be the property of a long, lanky gentleman with unfortunate sandy-coloured hair than of the young man in the striped silk coat. The four of them, the young man and his sister, the lanky gentleman and the plain lady, had had the appearance of forming a fairly, tight-knit group, for she had noticed that they had made up a party together for supper, and that while the plain young woman was dancing with the handsome young man, the handsome young man's sister, who was every bit as handsome as he, was partnering the lanky gentleman, and that both couples always stood together in the same set.

Thereafter, she had remarked them quite often. She had

seen them at church on Sunday morning, when they had been in the company of an older lady and gentleman, who, from the older lady's brilliant complexion and lustrous black curls, she had taken to be the parents of the young man and his sister. Another time, she had seen them in a box at the theatre, the young man modishly attired in a suit of purple cloth with cream satin waistcoat, his sister sparkling in rose-coloured silk with silver ribbons in her hair. She had seen the two younger ladies shopping together in the High Street, and almost bumped head-on into the young man, arm in arm with his lanky friend, strolling along the Royal Crescent. She had not noticed any of the younger folk taking the waters, but she had seen the older lady and gentleman do so, and could only conjecture that it was for the benefit of *their* health that the party was come to Cheltenham: the young man and his sister accompanying their parents, the lanky gentleman and the plain but agreeable lady presumably accompanying their two friends, for that they were acquaintances of long standing seemed obvious by the familiarity with which they treated one another.

Anne had neither schemed nor contrived for any sort of direct encounter—she would not have known how to set about doing so, even had she wished it. Her nature was too straightforward, there was nothing devious, nothing cunning, that could come to her aid in such a situation; but in truth she had been quite content to play the rôle of observer. It was fate which had decreed otherwise.

Coming one morning from the Pump Room, where she had seen all the members of the group save the young man himself, she had been roughly jostled by a party of young bucks crowding their way through the door. She had stumbled and would have fallen, had it not been for the sudden strength of a supporting arm, steadying her and bearing her up: the arm had belonged to the young man. He had evidently been on his way in to join the rest of his party, but he had stayed long enough at her side to check that she had taken no hurt—to express himself somewhat forcibly on the subject of "conceited jackanapes with no sense and fewer manners"—and finally, in response to her own murmured gratitude and Miss Morcomb's rather more volubly "thanking heavens that he had been there", to assure them that he had been only too glad to be of service.

She might quite reasonably, after that, without being in any way extravagant, have looked for some form of acknowledgement had they chanced to pass in the street: what she would not have dared to look for, nor even, in her wildest imaginings, to hope for, was that he should publicly approach her, in a crowded Assembly Room, and request the pleasure of her company. Yet so it had happened. The Master of Ceremonies had formally made the introductions—the young man was Mr Richard Wykeham, and he wished to be dancing with her. Was ever more confusion in any maidenly breast? How could she possibly tell him that her strength did not permit of dancing?—She could not; and, indeed, had lasted the length of not one but *two* whole sets without once feeling the need to be sitting down or passing out or taking in fresh air. She had been too intent on knowing herself the cynosure, if not quite of *all* eyes, at least of a great many.

Mr Wykeham had not been one who must be silent whilst he danced. He had kept up a lively flow of conversation, being flatteringly interested in Anne's situation—wishing to know whether this was her first visit to the spa, how long she remained, whether she was enjoying herself—at the same time as being amiably forthcoming as to his own. He had confirmed that he was here with his parents and sister, in order that his father, who tended to be a martyr to a faulty digestive system, might take the waters. His sister, Anne had learnt, was called Judith (another romantic name!) whilst the plain young lady and the lanky gentleman—childhood friends, as she had surmised—were a Miss Frances Thompson and a Mr Jack Meldrum. Mr Wykeham had confessed that he did not himself find Cheltenham to be perhaps the most *enthralling* place he had ever visited, but had said that nevertheless they were managing pretty successfully to keep themselves amused. There were plenty of good walks to be explored, plenty of interesting drives to be taken in the surrounding countryside. Possibly, one morning, Miss Fredericks might be prevailed upon to accompany them? He would have a word with his sister and ask her to arrange something at the first opportunity. To-morrow morning they were all booked for a ride; he did not know whether Miss Fredericks, by any chance, was a rider? Well, no matter! The morning after would do just as well. "Shall you be in the Pump Room? I will tell Judith that she is to introduce herself. I will give her strict instructions . . ."

Anne had waited in vain for Miss Wykeham to introduce herself: she never had. The "morning after" had come and gone, and the morning after that, as well. It was the last that Anne had ever seen of either Miss Wykeham or her brother. She had caught a brief glimpse of Miss Thompson, with Mr. Meldrum, in the Pump Room a day or so later, but had been far too shy to approach them; and the very next day afterwards had received an urgent message from Boswood, summoning her home. The message had surprised her, for Adam had been promising a visit so soon as Isabella had been safely brought to bed, an event which, according to all calculations, should have occurred several days since. It had been with no little trepidation, therefore, that Anne and Miss Morcomb had left their lodgings and set off post haste, into Oxfordshire. With dread had they reached Boswood—with fear descended from the carriage—only to find Isabella herself come running down the front steps to greet them, in the best of good health and eager to impart the information that she was now the mother of a *second* fine boy. The summons to return had not been on Isabella's behalf, but on Adam's. He had started out to see them and had suffered the misfortune—a not altogether uncommon one, it had to be said—of being stopped upon the road by a band of marauding footpads.

'They took nothing from him, for by a happy chance he had nothing worth their taking, but out of sheer malice they did him some injury—nothing too serious, I thank God, though had the shot gone any higher it must have took off his whole hand. As it is, he has had a most narrow escape, and one cannot be surprised if it has unnerved him. He has got it into his head that only at Boswood can we any of us be safe—nothing would do for it but that you and Miss Morcomb should be brought back home upon the instant. I would have interceded for you, only that he has worked himself into such a state . . . I do not doubt but that sooner or later he will come out of it, but for the moment I believe it will be best if we treat him gently and do nothing that is like to vex him. It seems only kind, after all that he has been through.'

Adam, alas, had not "come out of it". It had marked the beginning of his nervousness, of his general reluctance to let any of the family out of his sight, or to travel more than five miles in any direction from his home. Anne had had her brief interlude of romance; and with that, it seemed, she must be content for the rest of her life.

The carriage, now, was within the environs of Cheltenham. Another fifteen minutes—another ten—and they would be there. Anne opened her mouth to comment as such to Isabella, but before even a syllable could be got out there was the sound of a sharp report, as of a shot being fired, the heavy drumming of horse's hooves across the turf, and the shouted command to 'Stand!' The carriage jolted to a halt, almost throwing them off their seats. Isabella screamed, the door was thrown open, and Anne found herself confronted by the barrel of a pistol.

Surprisingly, she felt no immediate desire either to echo Isabella's scream nor to faint dead away; which in all probability, as she later averred, owed nothing whatsoever to any special quality of bravery or of cool-headedness which she might possess, but everything to her penchant for pursuing the trivial and the unimportant. In this instance, it was the nature of the command which was happily preoccupying her. "Stand" was the word which had been shouted. There was surely some deficiency here? Should not the expression be rather, Stand and *Deliver?* She was sure she had read somewhere that that was what the highwaymen were used to shout. "Stand and Deliver!"—for after all, it was the delivery in which they were mainly interested, was it not?

It seemed that it was not; or at any rate, not on this particular occasion, for so soon as Isabella could be induced to cease screaming, the heavily masked gentleman who had appeared in the doorway lowered his pistol, announced in civilised tones that he "had no quarrel with ladies", and earnestly craved their forgiveness for any alarm which may have been occasioned.

Anne found her tongue.

'Pray do not mention it, sir. I am sure there has been some genuine error.'

'There has indeed.' He spoke earnestly. 'Had I known whom—that is—that you were alone and unprotected—' Why did she have the impression that he had been about to say something different? Something that he had chosen at the last minute not to say?—'I should not have troubled you. I give you my word! It shall not occur again.'

A slight smile curved Anne's lips.

'You are too kind, sir!'

'There is no kindness in it. Simply, I repeat: I have no quarrel with members of your sex. I will beg your pardon once again for the interruption; and if you have no objections to make, shall be on my way.'

Anne said gravely that for her part she had not the least objection in the world. Isabella, transfixed, said nothing at all. The masked gentleman inclined his head.

'In that case, I will detain you no longer.—I take it you head for Cheltenham?'

The question seemed directed personally at Anne. She hesitated; and felt, rather than saw, the eyes behind the velvet mask subjecting her to scrutiny.

'For Cheltenham,' she said.

'Then I will bid you God speed. Ladies—' Lightly he raised a hand to the brim of his hat—'your servant.'

With that, he was gone. They heard another shouted instruction to their coachman, this time to "Drive on!", and the sound of hoofbeats receding across the turf whence they had come. By leaning forward on her seat, Anne was just able to make out a figure on horseback disappearing over the brow of the hill. She sat back, as the carriage jerked into motion.

'Well! There is an extraordinary adventure to befall us! Whatever is one to make of *that*, do you suppose?'

Isabella said nothing, save: 'I wish you had not told him where we were going. I wish you had not. Who knows but he may not be waiting for us somewhere further on upon the route? I wish you had told him we were going somewhere different. You might have said Bath just as well. We might quite easily have been going to Bath.'

'Except,' said Anne, 'that we are not upon the right road.'

'What is that to the point? At least he would not be waiting to pounce out upon us further on!'

Anne reflected.

'I hardly think it can be his intention to pounce a *second* time. He has said twice that he has no quarrel with ladies. Really, in view of his calling, one cannot but concede that he treated us with a quite uncommon degree of courtesy.'

'Oh, yes! To be sure!' Isabella spoke hysterically. 'Other than firing pistols over our heads and frightening us half to death, he did nothing at all that one should complain of.'

Anne laughed.

'And you are the one who is always hankering after excitement! Am I to infer that now you have encountered some you are not quite so keen as you were?'

'There is excitement,' said Isabella, 'and there is excitement. Being held up on the road by masked ruffians is not what I had in mind.'

'I will grant you that it is rather extreme. On the other hand, I am not entirely satisfied that *ruffian* is an accurate description. He had almost the air of a person of quality.'

'Oh! A perfect gentleman! If we had been members of his own sex he would doubtless have run us through, merely for the fun of it. As we are ladies, he fortunately contents himself with firing pistols over our heads and—'

'Yes, yes, and frightening us half to death! But only think what a splendid talking point it will prove!'

'There is that,' conceded Isabella. 'A talking point is always a useful thing to have, particularly when one is going amongst strangers.'

'So there you are, then! Just be thankful for small mercies. I declare I never knew anyone so ungrateful . . . a story such as this will very likely sustain you for the entire length of our stay!'

Cheltenham was reached without any further mishap. Mrs Gardner, every bit as hospitable as Anne remembered her to be, was waiting to greet them, and Patey, Isabella's personal maid, who had been sent on ahead the previous day, had their boxes already unpacked, brushes and combs already laid out upon the dressing table, flowers in a vase upon the window sill.

'It is all as cosy as can be,' declared Isabella, well satisfied. 'I am glad, after all, that we did not take lodgings in the High Street. I should not at all care to be in the midst of all that hustle and hubbub. I far prefer somewhere quiet, where one may have a bit of peace. And talking of peace, I must tell you, Mrs Gardner, that we had the most extraordinary experience on the way here—did we not, Anne? Was it not most extraordinary? A young man in a mask, firing pistols over our heads and frightening us half to death! And then, you know, just riding straight off again, without troubling himself even to take the rings from our fingers or the purses out of our pockets!'

'Oh, he never does! It's not his way.' Mrs Gardner shook her head. 'Never takes anything from anyone. The Perfect Gentleman, we call him. He's well known in these parts; quite an institution. You'll often hear folk say they've met the Perfect Gentleman out upon the road.'

'Well!' Isabella turned, triumphantly, to Anne. 'Is that not the very expression I used myself? Did I not say to you, that his manners were those of a perfect gentleman?'

'You did,' said Anne.

'I did!' Isabella switched back, with an air of confiding, to Mrs Gardner. 'I knew at once that he could not be any ordinary highwayman. He had that certain air about him—and then, the manner in which he apologised for having disturbed us! It really was quite charming—Was it not, Anne? The way he asked us if we had any objections to his taking his leave? Was it not charmingly done?'

'He was certainly at pains to assure himself we had suffered no permanent fright. But you say, Mrs Gardner, that he is well known? Does he never do more to his victims than fire pistols over their heads?'

'Not if they are ladies. If they are gentlemen, then he has the habit of requesting them to remove their gloves and shake him by the hand.'

'How very odd!' said Isabella.

'It's generally believed the poor gentleman is a little—' Mrs Gardner, significantly, tapped a finger to her head. 'Rumour has it he was crossed in love and that it has turned his mind. I wouldn't know whether that was true or not. But whichever way, he's harmless enough. There's none round here would ever seek to do him injury. I daresay, if you talk to people, you'll find several have had the privilege of being stopped by him. They've all got their stories to tell. But one thing they'll have in common: they'll all have been treated with perfect courtesy.'

Isabella waited until Mrs Gardner had closed the door.

'Well!' she said. 'Here is an excellent beginning to our stay! I have always been of the opinion that a little more excitement would not come amiss, and now, you see, we are having it—and in Cheltenham, of all places upon earth! You will agree, it is scarcely the hub of the universe. Indeed, I do not mind admitting *now* that I had secretly feared it might prove rather tame, and you know that I am one who can never have too much of the rough and tumble of life.—But I will tell you what: we had best not mention anything of this to our poor Adam. He is quite anxious enough on our behalf as it is. Only let him discover that we have had an encounter with a highwayman—albeit one who is a *perfect gentleman*—and he will be calling us back to Boswood straight away. Let us make a sacred, solemn pact that we will not tease him with it but keep it strictly *entre nous.*'

It was a pact to which Anne was only too willing to pledge herself: *she* had no desire to be rushing home again the very minute she had arrived. Besides, as Isabella sagely pointed out: 'It is entirely in his own best interests. He would only fret himself into a state. It would not be at all kind in us to worry him with it. In fact, it would be quite horridly selfish! Do you not agree?'

Anne did; and said so.

'I knew that you would,' said Isabella. 'That is what is so comforting . . . the fact that we are always in accord. I am so thankful, by the by—' she squeezed Anne's arm, encouragingly—'that this morning's incident did not frighten you too much. I know that you are not one for the mad excitements of life, as I am. I have been in the greatest fear lest it may have put you off.'

'Not at all,' said Anne. 'I assure you, a little excitement just now and again pleases me very well . . .'

CHAPTER THREE

Cheltenham might not, as Isabella had observed, be the hub of the universe, but still there were sufficient of the Polite World in evidence to speedily convince the newcomers of the urgent necessity to be refurbishing their wardrobes before venturing too prominently into public.

'It becomes borne in upon one,' said Isabella 'that what is the height of fashion in *Oxford* cannot be depended upon as being so elsewhere. I never felt such a dowdy in my life as when we passed those ladies in the High Street this morning . . . no wonder they stared! *I* should stare if I saw someone dressed so very odd. I positively shudder to think what sort of a picture we must present! Our hair is as much absurdly too *high* as our waists are a great deal too *low* . . . I cannot conceive how they ever came to be so!'

'Possibly,' ventured Anne, 'because it is where nature positioned them.'

'Oh! Nature! Nature has nothing whatsoever to do with

it. If it is the *fashion* to wear one's waist beneath one's armpits, then obviously that is where it must be worn. Unless, of course, one wishes to make oneself a laughing stock.'

'And yet I seem to recall,' murmured Anne, with a slight smile, 'that when we saw some ladies in Oxford walking about with their waists beginning almost before their bosoms had had a chance to finish, we were unkind enough to speculate whether they may not have been born with some hideous deformity.'

'That was before we knew it was the fashion. Now that we are aware, it behoves us to follow suit, else *we* shall be the ones who are in danger of being thought to have the deformity. It never does to stand out for the wrong reason—one would not care to present oneself as being in any way a different shape from the rest of society. For my part, I am already coming to think the new styles a vast deal improved upon the old.'

'The materials are certainly pretty,' said Anne. 'I particularly liked that pale lilac muslin that the one lady was wearing.'

'Yes, was it not enchanting! And would suit you admirably! It is exactly what you need, with your light colouring. Why do we not go out straight away and take a look at some? We passed a shop this morning where I believe I saw the very same thing at thirty-five shillings. I know that that is not what one would call a bargain, precisely, but after all one cannot expect to be in the fashion for nothing. It is just as well I cautioned you against buying that bonnet in Oxford! It would have been a sad waste of money, for pink satin would not go at all well with lilac muslin, and lilac muslin is what I am fully determined you shall have. There was also some very pretty lemon which would suit you, and a pale green which I am not so sure about, although there is no way of really telling for certain until one has examined it close to and tried it up against you in the light . . . why do we not go immediately and do so? We are under no obligation to buy, and there can be no harm in just looking.'

Anne agreed that there could not. For all that she was nearly four and twenty and fast approaching middle age, for all the bad habits that she had fallen into of putting herself down, of laughing at her own pretensions, she was by no means averse to looking as pretty as nature would allow. Money was not lacking—she had a competence of her own, inherited upon the death of her parents—and neither was taste. She knew well enough what became her and what did not, and despite initial reservations about a waist which began "almost before the bosom had had a chance to finish" could not but acknowledge that the flimsy fabrics and pastel shades of the new fashions were flattering to one of her slender physique and delicate complexion: it needed very little encouragement from her sister-in-law before she was acquiring a whole new wardrobe for herself.

Clear muslin dresses might be had for as little as seven and sixpence—the temptation proved irresistible! Real Indian muslin at thirty-five shillings the yard must be treated with more caution, but both the lilac and the lemon proved far too enticing (and paid her far too great a compliment when tried up against her) to be denied. She purchased lengths of each and arranged to have them run up as soon as possible, whilst Isabella, whose colouring was bolder and figure more robust, was seduced by an apple green silk and a vividly printed chintz; all of which, quite naturally, necessitated further purchases, by way of slippers and gloves, to offset them. Slippers and gloves in *their* turn must needs have shawls and bonnets to go with them; and of what use were new bonnets, Isabella wished to know, if they were to be perched on top of old hairstyles? No use at all! They would look quite ridiculous. New hairstyles must be acquired as well, if they were to avoid the dread stigma of being a laughing stock.

New hairstyles, accordingly, were organised. Anne felt herself a stranger, at first, with curls cut close to her head and clustered on her brow, but soon came to feel the advantages of it: there was a freedom, a lightness, which had not been there before.

'So much more refreshing!' Isabella ran ecstatic hands through new-cropped hair. 'How glad I am that we are come to Cheltenham! Now we may go out and about and feel ourselves the equal of all.'

It could not but be a strange sensation for Anne, to be retracing almost exactly the steps of five years previously. *Then* she had been nineteen; subdued, to be sure, by the double blow of bereavement and her own recent illness, but nonetheless with that unquenchable optimism which is the property of youth. At nineteen almost anything might happen—and, indeed, most probably will. At four and twenty, she had learnt not to expect too much from life. She had trained herself to be content, and had thought that she was so. It took Cheltenham, and a new mode of dressing, to open her eyes to the truth. She was *not* content! She longed just as eagerly for romance now as ever she had at the age of nineteen. Optimism might have been dampened by the intervening years of confinement at Boswood, but hope was not yet dead. It quickened within her each time that she regarded her new image in the glass—each time that she set foot in the street, or caught a glimpse in the distance of a young man with dark hair . . .

With that asperity which now came rather too naturally to her in her dealings with herself, she lost no time in administering a series of sharp set-downs. What folly at her time of life to be sighing after a young man who would very probably not recognise her if he passed within inches! And even if he did—even if he went so far as to accord her a bow of acknowledgement and a "Good day"—what, pray, would it profit her? It would be very surprising (blushing at the indelicacy of her own speculations) if he were not long since become a married man and the proud father of a whole nurseryful of little ones. Besides, what reason for assuming that *he* should be back in Cheltenham only because *she* was? It was hardly to be supposed that his papa would come every season to try the waters, and even less to be supposed that his son would be always accompanying him. Married men had responsibilities towards their wives and children.

With such sobering reflections did she seek to quell her yearnings: the effect was minimal. She might tell herself as repeatedly as she chose that Richard Wykeham had not only never considered her as being of the slightest importance in his life (had he not demonstrated the fact in most conclusive fashion by his abrupt departure from the scene five years earlier?) but would not be likely to remember either her name or even the very fact of her existence—she might remind herself incessantly of her own advancing years and the interval of time which must assuredly have wrought changes in *his* situation—still it did nothing to quench that air of expectation which had assailed her on the journey here, and had persisted in despite of all her admonitions: the fires had been rekindled and would not easily be damped.

One morning, on arriving back at their lodgings from the Pump Room (where Anne had been looking in vain for a glimpse of any familiar face, and Isabella with rather more success for families with whom she might strike up an instant friendship: she had found no less than three during the course of one short hour) they were greeted by Mrs Gardner with the promising intelligence that "a gentleman" had called to see them and had left his card. Anne's heart, at this, had beat a little faster—how could it do otherwise? They knew no gentleman! Had no acquaintances of any kind! Unless—

'Here is a coincidence!' cried Isabella. 'Sir Tristram is in town!'

Anne turned away. Calmly, she began to untie the strings on her bonnet.

'Sir Tristram?'

'Yes, indeed! Sir Tristram Eve—is that not a happy coincidence? Although, as I now recall, he has an estate somewhere nearby, so possibly it is no coincidence at all but a perfectly natural occurrence which we might have expected, had we only stopped to think about it . . . I wonder if perhaps Adam may not have wrote to him and mentioned that we were to be here? Most likely that will be the way things fell out. He will have informed him of our arrival and Sir Tristram will have decided to call upon us—and just at a time when we are most in need of it, for try as I might I cannot seem able to meet up with anyone who has sons of marriageable age. Could anything be more fortuitous? Let us hope he repeats his visit very speedily, before we attend at the Rooms . . . it would be a distinct advantage if you were to go there already assured of a partner, and I think you will own that Sir Tristram is by no means to be despised! Even apart from the fact of his title, he is a very acceptable figure of a man. I am sure that *I* should not object to dance with him!'

Anne should not object, either; but neither could she be excited. Certainly it was no fault of Sir Tristram's that his name was not Richard. She did not hold *that* against him. Indeed, she did not specifically hold anything against him, other than that she wished he might be somebody else. As he was not, however, she supposed it would be ungracious not to show proper gratitude for his attentions; and certainly, as Isabella said, it would be a distinct advantage to make her first appearance in the Rooms already assured of a partner. She would not a second time wish to be relegated to the rôle of spectator.

When Sir Tristram presented himself at their lodgings the next day, therefore, Anne was as happy to see him as she ought to have been; and if not quite in the same raptures as Isabella when upon his taking his leave he asked if he might have the pleasure of engaging her for that evening, was at any rate very well satisfied with the prospect of being able to stand up, even if it were (the thought came to her, unbidden) only Sir Tristram. He could never be a favourite with her—she was not sure why. She was used to consider her feelings with some care before pronouncing any judgement as to like or dislike, yet with Sir Tristram she could not make up her mind with any certainty as to the one or to the other. He visited occasionally at Boswood—virtually the only visitor they ever saw, apart from Isabella's mama. He was an acquaintance—she would put it no stronger—of Adam's. His address was good, his manner civil, and his face and person both more than tolerable (if one could forgive the minor defect of his happening to have hair that was of a brownish hue rather than a particular shade of black). Still, she could not positively make up her mind to like him.

In the meantime, it had to be admitted that it was vastly agreeable to be dancing again, and feeling herself, if not quite back in the days of her young girlhood, to be at any rate far less of a maiden aunt than of recent years. Sir Tristram congratulated her upon her dress (it was the pale lilac with a lemon sash, and a simple lilac ribbon threaded through her hair).

'These new fashions do not become everyone. There are some whose shape can only benefit from concealment—to reveal them at all is practically a crime against mankind. *Others*, by contrast, can scarcely be revealed too much.' His eye lingered a moment, appreciatively, upon Anne's person. 'I do not need to tell you in which category I consider *you* to belong.'

Once, such a compliment (accompanied as it was by such a glance) would have burned Anne's pale cheek a painful scarlet. Now, she only inclined her head in graceful acknowledgement and turned it off with a murmured reference to the air of Cheltenham being "very beneficial to one's looks".

'It would certainly seem to be proving itself so in your case. I have never before seen you so animated. You do not mind my saying so? It has often concerned me that your brother keeps you so close. His disposition is nervous, I know, but when all is said and done, no harm can befall a person in Cheltenham—not that that will stop the poor fellow teasing himself almost into an apoplexy. I will tell you what, Miss Fredericks! I have business in that direction very shortly. How if I were to call in upon him at Boswood and report how you do?'

'That would be most kind. I am sure he would welcome any first-hand news.'

'Oh, I will set his mind at rest . . . I will tell him in what good looks I have found you!—I will also tell him, whilst I am about it, what I think of his action—or lack of action—in not troubling himself to inform me that you were here!'

An inquiring frown wrinkled Anne's brow.

'Was it not from him that you heard it?'

'No, indeed! I was left to find out for myself. Fortunately I make a point of always scanning the newspapers to discover what new arrivals there might be. Had I not done so I may very well have missed you, which I assure you would have vexed me exceedingly.'

His eye, once again, rested upon her. He seemed inclined to play the lover—a rôle he had been so far from assuming on his rare visits to Boswood that she had sometimes been in two minds whether he had even been aware of her presence. She was feminine enough to enjoy the sensation of being flirted with, whilst at the same time being quite unable to take it seriously. Lighthearted dalliance was not in her nature; she must either be embarrassed by it, or amused. At the age of nineteen she could only have been embarrassed: at the age of twenty-four, she had sufficient command over herself to opt for amusement, merely returning his innuendo with a composed smile and a little shake of the head.—It was as well, perhaps, for her peace of mind, that she was in utter ignorance of the transforming properties of a new hair style: the *composed smile,* intended rather to convey benevolence than actively to encourage, had exactly the opposite effect to that which its bestower fondly imagined; whilst the little shake of the head which accompanied it, far from being in any way admonitory, nor even just faintly chiding, was imbued with an air of positive roguishness.

'And how do you care for Cheltenham?' Sir Tristram posed the question with polite formality: his eye, however, still lingered. 'Do you find it to your taste?'

'Very much so,' said Anne. 'I like it very well.'

'It is not too quiet for you? Too lacking in adventure?'

'Oh! My sister-in-law will tell you, I am not one who is for ever on the lookout for noise and bustle. As for adventure, I believe we had sufficient on the way here to last us a lifetime.'

'Indeed?' Sir Tristram raised an eyebrow. 'You met with some mishap?'

'I am not sure that I should call it a mishap, exactly—in fact, now that I come to think of it I am not sure that I should call it anything at all, for Isabella and I have pledged ourselves to strictest secrecy on the subject for fear lest it reach the ears of my brother and throw him into one of his frights.'

'But you cannot suppose that *I* would turn traitor and betray you? The last thing I would wish is to have you whisked back again to Boswood! Have I not already said, that I will set his mind at rest? Come, Miss Fredericks! You have whetted my appetite . . . what is this adventure which is not to be called a mishap?'

'Well, I will trust you to keep the secret, since gentlemen are commonly held to be reliable in such matters—but mind, you must not let me down!'

Sir Tristram bowed.

'You have my word on it.'

'That is a great relief! I do not mind confessing,' said Anne, 'that I am near to bursting point with keeping silent . . . the only person in whom we have confided is our landlady, Mrs Gardner, and *she*, so far from being properly impressed and falling instantly into hysterics on our behalf, calmly informs us that it is not at all an extraordinary experience in these parts, but on the contrary may almost be said to be *common*place . . . a sad let down! The fact of the matter is that our carriage was held up on the road by a most curiously polite gentlemen. He not only apologised profusely for disturbing us, but actually went on his way without taking so much as a single trinket!!'

'Ah, yes . . . the Perfect Gentleman! He is quite a familiar figure.'

'That is what our landlady said. I believe there is some tale attaching to him? A misfortune in love, according to Mrs Gardner.'

'That, if I may say so without offense, Miss Fredericks, is an explanation entirely typical of your sex . . . your minds must always be running on romance!'

'And the minds of yours,' returned Anne, cordially, 'on fighting and shooting . . . but let us not start a debate! Tell me instead about this *Perfect Gentleman* whom you all seem so anxious to claim as a celebrity.'

'There is not a great deal to tell other than that he has been at his work for the past several years and is quite obviously ripe for the asylum.'

'What makes you say so?'

Sir Tristram shrugged a shoulder.

'The fact would seem self-evident . . . anyone who spends the greater part of his time continually rampaging the same stretch of countryside holding up carriages to no purpose can scarcely be considered sane in any accepted sense of the term.'

'But might it not be that he is in search of one particular person? Mrs Gardner was telling us that it is his practice, whenever he meets up with *gentlemen*, to request them to remove their gloves and to shake him by the hand. Does this not signify to you that he is searching for some sign—some tell-tale mark?'

'Does it you?' said Sir Tristram, sounding amused.

'Oh, yes! It struck me immediately, for unless, as you say, the poor man is completely unhinged—'

'Which he almost certainly is. But supposing him for a moment, for the sake of argument, *not* to be—what kind of sign or mark had you in mind?'

'Ah! There you have me! I am not well versed in the Gothic art . . . how about a ring? Would that not do?'

'A ring?' Sir Tristram spread his hands. On one finger was a heavy silver signet of intricate design. 'Such as this, perhaps?'

'The very thing! It is both eye-catching and unmistakable . . . obviously the key to some past mystery! Tell me, Sir Tristram—' Anne's grey eyes sparkled mischievously. 'Has the Perfect Gentleman ever held up *your* carriage by any chance?'

'I have to confess that I have not so far had that honour. Would you advise me for the future to take the precaution of—ah—removing the bauble before undertaking any sort of journey?'

'I should say that it would quite definitely be advisable, for who knows but he may not turn nasty when once he comes up against the object that he is looking for?'

'And you conjecture that this ring of mine may be that object . . . yes! I perceive there is some logic in your argument. *Female* logic, of course—'

'But of course!'

'Still, one would not wish to be caught with the incriminating evidence upon one's person. What would you suppose, Miss Fredericks, it is incriminating *of*?'

'Oh! I daresay at some time or another you will have done

him some misservice—all unaware, naturally, or you would not still be wearing your ring, which is the only means by which he may recognise you—and he has sworn eternal vengeance and is out to bring you to book at all costs. How does that strike you for a good plot?'

'It strikes me as being an excellent example of that Gothic art in which you profess yourself not well versed . . . highly ingenious and in the last degree improbable! This wretched fellow engrosses everyone's attention. All the ladies are wild for him. You are all convinced he is a figure of thwarted romance and would like nothing better than to enfold him in a maternal embrace and seek to bring him solace.'

'Now you go too far!' objected Anne. 'I am sure I said nothing about embracing him, maternally or any other wise.'

'Do not attempt to deny it! You are all of you the same. You will take any lame duck beneath your wing and smother it with your caresses. We poor, dull, everyday mortals who choose *not* to race about the roads with masks covering our faces are at a sad disadvantage.'

'Yes,' said Anne. '*You* have not been crossed in love and driven stark mad.'

'Neither has he, Miss Fredericks! Have we not just this minute established that his sole motive is one of revenge? For a wrong that was done him unintentionally? *That* is hardly very romantic, I think you will agree!'

'It would certainly be interesting to meet him face to face and find out.'

'Would it not,' said Sir Tristram. 'Would it not . . . I fancy *some* of us would be in for a sad disillusionment. But I am sick of talking of the fellow! Let us talk of something more pleasant—yourself, for example. You are here for a month, I believe your sister-in-law said. How do you propose to keep yourself amused during all that time? Cheltenham, I fear, is not London—there is not a constant round of entertainment to be choosing from. There are, on the other hand, a fair number of pleasant excursions which may be taken. Have you explored at all? I should be very willing to act as your guide. In fact, I was going to suggest, if it should be convenient, that I might call upon you tomorrow morning and take yourself and Mrs Fredericks for a drive.—Would that suit? Should you find it agreeable? We might go wherever you chose. I do not know whether you have any particular preferences?'

Even as she indicated that she did not—that she should be quite content to place herself in his hands and allow him to pick the route—she was reminded of that other time, when a certain Mr Wykeham, whose name was Richard, had pledged himself to take her on a similar expedition. If he had only redeemed that pledge, would her life have turned out any different? She could not but suppress a small sigh.—Sir Tristram, noticing, was instantly on the alert. Was she feeling tired? Had he wearied her? Should she care to sit down?—Anne, feeling her own lack of manners, reassured him. She was not in the least bit tired and neither had he wearied her. If anyone were to be weary, she should sooner suppose it to be him, allowing her to rattle on as he had. As for sitting down, there could be no question.

'This is the first ball I have been to in a great many years . . . you may imagine how I am determined on savouring every single second of it!'

'But you sighed!'

'Merely for the passage of time . . . I was foolishly letting myself dwell upon the last occasion that I was here. The older I grow, the more convinced I become that it is a great mistake to indulge in the luxury of memory: it can serve only to heighten one's awareness of one's own deterioration!'

'I cannot think why it should—certainly it cannot in *your* case. I am persuaded that you can have changed hardly at all in five short years, and even if you have, it can only have been a change for the better. *Then* you would have been but an unformed girl. *Now*—'

She did not hear what he had to say about now. She was trying to recall whether she had told him the date of her previous visit—she was inclined to believe she had not. Very possibly Isabella may have done so, however. Her sister-in-law was always a more generous dispenser of information than the more reticent Anne.

'Delicate looks such as yours can only be enhanced by

the passing of the years: it is the sort of beauty which time augments rather than shatters.'

Belatedly, she became aware that Sir Tristram was paying her another of his compliments, that it behove her to be smiling and shaking her head, not wrinkling her brow in the vain pursuit of trivialities. The moment had passed, however: the set was already come to an end and she was being led back again across the floor to Isabella, obstinately seated amongst the ranks of plump, middle-aged matrons and raddled dowagers.

'A mother of two has no business to be dancing. Let the gentlemen be shared out amongst those who have most need of them. I could not bear to think that *I* was the cause of ruining some young person's chances.'

'I wish that you had joined us!' Anne slid down, fanning herself, into the vacant seat beside her. 'There are several ladies far older than you, and if *they* have no objection to ruining a young person's chances, I am sure I cannot see why you should . . . do say that next time you will take part! I hate to be standing up all by myself.'

'As a matter of fact—' Isabella glanced over her shoulder and dropped her voice conspiratorially to a half whisper as Sir Tristram turned away to pay his respects to an elderly dowager in a plum-coloured turban. 'I would not say so in front of Sir Tristram, but as matter of fact I am very glad that I did *not* join you . . . do not look now, but there is a young man opposite has been fixing you with his eye these past fifteen minutes or more. Seated where I am, I have been able to enjoy a clear and unobstructed view of him. He has never once let you out of his sight! As to who he might be, I have not the least idea, for unfortunately neither of my neighbours ever remembers to have seen him before, but I can tell you that he is quite excessively handsome!—Had he been plain, you know, I should not have bothered to mention it. There are quite enough *plain* young men about the place without going out of one's way to draw attention to them. As it is—' She suddenly broke off and clutched at Anne's arm. 'For goodness' sake, do not look! He is starting to move!—I have the feeling that he is coming this way—

he is certainly heading in this general direction . . . heavens above! He is making straight for us! I do believe it is his intention to stop and speak—what an extraordinary thing! Ten to one he has mistaken you for some other lady. That is what it will be. He thinks that you are someone he has met before . . . yes! He is approaching with quite an air of confidence. What a let down it will be, when he discovers he is in error!—If you are very quick you may risk a glance—now, whilst we are sheltered by the crowd—'

Obediently, Anne raised her eyes. For all that she was four and twenty and had learnt not to blush, she felt the colour suffusing her cheeks.—The young man stopped before them.

There was a pause; then: 'Miss Fredericks?' he said.

'Mr Wykeham,' murmured Anne.

CHAPTER FOUR

'To have been here but the one short month and to have no less than *two* eligible gentlemen vying with each other for your favours is, let me tell you, a feat by no means to be sneered at!'

Isabella spoke scoldingly. Anne, her head bent over her netting box, only smiled very slightly and said nothing.

'You may choose,' said Isabella, 'to think that I am romancing, but you have not my experience in these matters . . . I never saw a man so deep in love as Mr Wykeham! You may very probably not have noticed, you are always so determined on being sensible. Very likely *you* would not notice if he were to fall on his knees and make you a proposal—or if you did, you would only laugh and turn it aside. You would be bound to find *some* common sensical excuse for what you would call his irrational behaviour . . . you would say, I do not doubt, that he must have tripped over and caught himself a blow on the head which had temporarily deranged him . . . something of that nature. But you may take my word for it that sooner or later it is precisely what he *will* do—unless, of course, Sir Tristram steals a march on him. I am not so sure,' said Isabella, thoughtfully, 'of Sir Tristram. Last week I would have been prepared to swear that he regarded Mr Wykeham as a rival, for he stood all evening by my side whilst you were dancing together and positively refused to stand up with anyone else, even though I pointed out that there was a whole host of young ladies who had been left sitting down for want of any partner. In other circumstances I should have counted it excessively bad manners, but in a lover one is prepared to overlook almost anything, so long as it is consistent with the state of being in love. It put me strongly in mind of Mr Wykeham, that first evening, when he did nothing but stare! *He* might have had his choice amongst at least a dozen tolerable young women, but you see he would not: he was too intent upon pursuing *you*.—I suppose you would put *that* down to some oddity in your dress or your hairstyle. Or some oddity in *him*. You could never allow it to be natural reluctance on the part of a normal, susceptible young man to be letting a pretty girl out of his sight before he had had a chance to renew his acquaintance with her. *That* would not be rational.'

Again, Anne said nothing. Again, she smiled; except that this time it was a smile not so much of amusement as of recollection—sweet recollection, if the sweetness of the smile were anything to go by. She was by no means so determinedly common sensical as she would make herself out to be. If she had had any doubts that first evening—for the dialogue, in front of Isabella, had had of necessity to be circumscribed: *she* had been bashful, whilst *he* had been awkward—such doubts had long since been dispelled. Richard himself had taken very good care to do the dispelling.

'I could not bear the thought of losing you again! I had visions of your suddenly disappearing as you did before . . . I hunted for you high and low, made inquiries of everyone I met, whether they were acquainted with a Miss Fredericks . . . there was simply no tracing you! You cannot imagine the anguish that it caused me, knowing that I had failed to keep what *I*, at any rate, had regarded as a firm engagement.

The circumstances were beyond my control, but that was no consolation :if I could not find you to offer my apologies . . . all these years I have tortured myself, wondering what you must have thought!'

She did not tell him what she had thought, which was nothing more flattering to herself than that the engagement had slipped his mind and she along with it; neither did *he* attempt any explanation as to what the circumstances were which were "beyond my control". Anne wondered, but did not ask. After all this time, it could hardly be considered as of any importance. What *was* of importance was that he had been conscious of his failure—had sought for her, remembered her—and recognised. Perhaps Sir Tristram's gallantry had been no mere empty flattery after all. She was encouraged, at least, to believe that she had not changed quite as much as she had feared.

It was Richard who had changed; she could not but notice it (any more than she could help but think of him as Richard). If physically there had been no material alteration, other than the etching in of a few extra lines—the slight hardening of the jaw, a new firmness about the mouth—mentally the intervening years would seem to have taken their toll. He was no longer the carefree youth with whom she had fancied herself in love. No longer, as they danced, did he maintain a stream of vivacious talk, intended to divert and amuse. He had become more intense, more brooding, as if life had ceased to be the plaything of an idle hour, which once it had been.

At first, she had attributed his new-found gravity to that one reason which she most dreaded to hear confirmed—that he was no more a bachelor. Such, however, was not the case: he remained unmarried. Neither nagging wife nor the cares of domesticity could be held responsible for his changed demeanour. The cause, if cause there was, must be sought elsewhere. She could only conclude that he had suffered a disappointment in love. Sir Tristram might say what he would about "such being an explanation entirely typical of your sex": she would challenge him to find any other that was even half as convincing. Young men of light-hearted temperament, such as Richard's had been, did not grow solemn overnight for such trivial cares as having run themselves into debt or gambled away the family fortune. To fail at cards was an inconvenience which might easily be shrugged off: one's luck would surely change upon the morrow. To fail in *love* was a tragedy which must be both more wounding in its immediate impact and more lasting in its general effect. One could not recover all in an instant. Isabella was too precipitous!

Anne smiled again; a small, secretive, half smile, intended only for herself. One could not recover in an instant; but given time, and help, and just the slightest measure of encouragement . . .

'You are laughing again,' said Isabella. 'I suppose you think I am a poor, pea-brained creature who can never set eyes on a handsome man but has to fancy him in love with someone . . . well! You will learn. One of these days—you will see whether I am right. It will be a very great pity if I cannot prevail upon Adam to allow us another week or two, for I feel tolerably certain that that is as much time as Mr *Wykeham* needs to take the plunge. Sir Tristram may need rather longer. I own I was somewhat amazed that he should choose this particular time to go gallivanting off to London—one would have thought he would sooner remain here where he may keep an eye on Mr Wykeham. I am sure *I* should not run off and leave the field clear for a rival! On the other hand, of course, if he is to call in upon Adam on the way back, I daresay he feels that he will be gaining favour in your eyes, and that is a *very* loverlike sort of thing to wish for. On the whole, I am inclined to believe that another week or two would bring Sir Tristram to a head, as well. I do wish you would give me some indication as to which of the two you would prefer! It is no use trying to be modest and pretend the situation does not exist, for I am happy to say that it *does*. It is precisely the very reason that I brought you to Cheltenham in the first place. I told you, do you remember, that I was determined on finding a husband for you?'

Anne kept her eyes demurely on the work that she was doing.

'I remember . . . and my answer, as I recall, was that I

was very well content with the way things were?'

'And *mine,* as *I* recall, was poppycock!—or words to that effect. I daresay it is very vulgar in me to be so openly scheming and contriving, but you have no mama to do it for you, and since you are the last person on earth to make shift for yourself . . . the fact is,' said Isabella, bluntly, 'that you cannot go on living confined at Boswood, or you will grow old and crabby before your time, just as my great Aunt Eliza did, and all because she refused to marry a man with a squint! Well! Neither Mr Wykeham nor Sir Tristram can be said to suffer from *that* defect. In fact, neither of them could be said to suffer from any defect at all. They are both as fine as can be, and I am not in the least surprised you cannot choose between them. I should be hard put to do so myself.—What are you smiling at? Is it something I have said? If it is Great Aunt Eliza who amuses you, I assure you it was no amusement for those who had to live with her. The crossest old stick alive!—and so will you become if you do not start seriously to consider your future. I do not pretend the choice is easy, for I have already allowed that it is not. Sir Tristram, of course, has the advantage of a title, but then titles are not everything and no one can deny that Mr Wykeham comes from a most respectable family—there have been Wykehams in Yorkshire since I do not know when. Also, he is younger and by far the more handsome, although that is not *necessarily* to be counted as an advantage. Not when it comes to matrimony. An older man may frequently make the better husband, and good looks can sometimes grow decidedly tiresome, especially if one is leading any sort of social life. One has always to bear in mind that what has proved a Fatal Attraction to oneself will be all too likely to prove so to others, as well. Taken all in all, I am tempted to think that perhaps Sir Tristram—and yet I do not know! There is a something about Mr Wykeham . . . it is most unfortunate that he is at outs with his papa. It makes one hesitate, lest he comes from a family which is congenitally fractious. On the other hand, young men and their papas are for ever coming to blows over the merest trifles, and as the estate is entailed there can be no danger of his being cut off. That was one of the first things I looked into.

Not that one wishes to be *mercenary*, but—'

Anne was looking up, a frown creasing her brow.

'Did you say that R—Mr Wykeham!—is at outs with his papa?'

'Why, yes! It is common knowledge—I have been asking around. It seems they have not spoke to one another for the past five years. According to Mrs Truscott, who is the lady whose husband has the gout whom I was speaking with the other day in the Pump Room—do you remember? The lady in the hideous puce gown? Of course she is too old to be caring about whether she is in the fashion or not. She must be fifty if she is a day. It seems she comes here regularly, every season, and knows everybody there is to know and all their business, besides. She used to be acquainted with Mr Wykeham's mama, until they stopped coming. I suppose, after the accident, it became too painful.'

'Accident?' said Anne. 'What accident is that?'

'Why, the accident to Mr Wykeham's sister! Did you not know of it? Oh! It was the most terrible tragedy! Mrs Truscott was telling me. It seems they had gone out into the country for a ride with some friends when some drunken brute in a cart appeared out of nowhere, driving at heaven knows how many miles to the hour, and caused Miss Wykeham's horse to bolt. There was nothing that anyone could do—she was thrown before they could reach her. And the worst of it was, the creature who did it was never brought to book! Is it not always the way? The innocent must suffer whilst the wicked go scot free. It is what I am for ever saying: there is no justice in the world.'

Anne's face, which only seconds before had been most becomingly tinged with pink, had of a sudden grown very pale. She set down her netting.

'Miss Wykeham—' the words came out almost in a whisper. 'She was not—'

'Killed.' Isabella nodded, dramatically. 'They carried her straight way to the nearest hostelry, but she died before the night was out. According to Mrs Truscott, poor Mr Wykeham—that is, *our* Mr Wykeham, not his papa—went almost out of his mind with the anguish of it. It seems it was his horse that she was riding, and that in a moment of crisis it proved too strong for her. His papa holds him to blame, which is maybe the reason for their being no longer on terms. For my part, I would say it was the fault of the drunken brute in the cart. It is quite monstrous the way some of these smart young bucks think it clever to crack along at the most fearsome pace when they are so befuddled with brandy they could not even *walk* in a straight line, let alone *drive* in one. That is where your brother is in the right of it: he will never touch a drop if he is going to drive. Not' (with a sigh) 'that he ever does so, these days. However, that is beside the point. We were talking of Mr Wykeham and how he has had to bear the brunt. Mrs Truscott says that he has scarcely been seen in society from that day to this.—Rumour has it that the poor boy was driven stark mad and has had to be confined for reason of his own safety, but I pay no attention to gossip of *that* sort. As far as I am concerned, he is as sane as you or I. Not but what I should sympathise with him if he had—' She broke off. 'My dearest Anne! Whatever is the matter? You have turned positively as white as a sheet . . . my prattle has surely not upset you?'

'No—not at all.' Anne made an effort to speak naturally. 'It is only that I—I had not realised—'

And not realising, had committed a blunder of the first magnitude.

'I am sure that your *sister*—' she heard herself saying it: lightly, teasingly, spurred almost to coquettishness by her own inward rejoicing at the discovery of his still being single—'I am sure that your *sister* has long since ceased to be mere *Miss Wykeham* and has become something a great deal more grand!'

He had allowed a fractional pause before replying; and then, in tones which even at the time had struck her as being strangely devoid of emotion: 'You are wrong,' he had said. 'My sister never married.'

She could not blame him for not opening her eyes to the truth: a ballroom was no place for the breaking of such a piece of news as Isabella had just let slip. Neither could she blame him for never since reverting to the subject. She had seen for herself the closeness of the relationship which had existed between brother and sister—she could imagine all too vividly how the loss must have affected him.

A tide of crimson engulfed her. She put up both hands, to cover her face. So much for feminine intuition! How puny must her "disappointment in love" be made to seem, when set beside this so much starker tragedy. Small wonder the Richard Wykeham who had caused such flutterings in the breast of Anne Fredericks at the age of nineteen was a far different man from the one who had sought her out again at the age of twenty-four.

'I see that I ought not to have spoke,' said Isabella. 'It has obviously upset you. However' (reverting to her former tone of scolding) 'it is entirely your own fault! If you will not make your feelings known, then how is one to avoid trampling on them?'

'Indeed, you have trampled upon nothing—there is nothing to trample upon! It is only—'

'Only that you are determined on being in love with no one and allowing no one to be in love with you! You have given yourself away, however! Your secret is out! And now that I know where your preference lies—' Isabella broke off in some exasperation as there came a tap at the door. 'Really! Must one *always* be interrupted just as one is about to enjoy a good coze?—Yes, Betty! What is it?'

It was Sir Tristram, back again in Cheltenham and eager to pay his respects. Isabella clicked her tongue.

'Quel ennui! I suppose you had better invite him to step up. One can hardly—' turning to Anne, as the door closed—'say that we are not at home. He would know at once that it was not true, and besides he will have news from Boswood. I shall like to hear how the children go on.'

For Anne, the interruption was welcome rather than not—even if it *were* only Sir Tristram. A good coze with her sister-in-law was what she would wish to be avoiding at all costs. Isabella was one of the sweetest-natured souls on earth, but neither tact nor descretion could be said to have any place amongst her many virtues: with the best will in the world, she was not able to be silent.

Sir Tristram came to them directly from Boswood, bearing a letter from Adam.

'I thought that I would take the opportunity to deliver it straight away.'

'How very kind of you!' said Isabella.

'No kindness, I assure you . . . self-indulgence, I should rather call it! I have been but five days away, and it has seemed at times more like fifty.' He bestowed a meaningful glance upon Anne as he spoke. She smiled, dutifully, and murmured words to the effect that she was sure London must be very enervating and that everyone must always be glad to return home from it.

'It is not only returning *home*. Just at present there are other attractions in Cheltenham for me besides that.'

'One of which must be some refreshment at the end of your journey! What may we offer you? Will you take a glass of sherry and a biscuit?' Determinedly, Anne steered the conversation into less dangerous channels. Sir Tristram's gallantry had long since ceased to flatter: she began to find it an embarrassment.

Isabella, meanwhile, had been briefly running her eye over the contents of Adam's letter. Now, she made a small moue of dissatisfaction and handed the page over to Anne.

'Here! You had better read what he says.'

Anne took the page, wonderingly. It seemed that Adam had said something to vex—she quickly discovered what it was.

My dear Isabella, he wrote, in his customary thin, rather cramped hand. *I have considered your application to be allowed to remain longer in Cheltenham but have regretfully to inform you that I cannot feel it to be a feasible proposition. You have now been four weeks away, and the children begin to have need of you. Also, there is Anne to be thought of. Her constitution is not so robust as yours—she cannot be doing with the amount of excitement that YOU can take. All in all, I believe it will be best if you return the last of the month, as arranged. To this end, Sir Tristram has very generously offered to convey you in his own carriage; an offer which I have had no hesitation in accepting on your behalf. I shall expect you to be back with us some time this coming week, and will await your arrival with impatience. Believe me, your loving husband, etc.*

There was a pause. Sir Tristram spread his hands.

'I am sorry,' he said, 'if the news disappoints.'

'It ought not,' said Isabella, 'but I will not conceal that it does. One had hoped that with the added weight of *your* supplication he might have been prevailed upon to grant us our extension.'

'I promise you that I did my best. I assured him that I had left Miss Fredericks in the most blooming of health, but I fear he will not be happy until you are both safely returned to him.—Has he mentioned, by the by, that I am to take you in my carriage?'

'He has,' said Isabella. 'We are most grateful.'

'You must not be downcast, you know. What has been engineered once may the more easily be engineered a second time—and a third, and a fourth, until in the end there is no engineering needed at all. He will soon grow accustomed, and lose his fears.'

'I sincerely trust that you are right,' said Isabella. She looked across, apologetically, at Anne. 'In the meantime, I am afraid, it would seem that we must abandon all the grand schemes that we have made.'

'Oh, I daresay we shall manage to survive!' Anne spoke with a lightness she was far from feeling. She had been counting, just as much as Isabella, on an extension being granted them: the blow of its being withheld was something she could not yet come to grips with. On Friday, Richard had been going to drive them out to Tewkesbury. How was she to break it to him, that now they should be unable to go? How was she—

'To-night, Miss Fredericks?'

Too late, she become aware that Sir Tristram was addressing her.

'I beg your pardon! I was not properly attending.'

'The fault was mine.—The speediness of your recall must raise a thousand problems to occupy you. I was merely inquiring whether you attend the Rooms this evening, and if so whether I might solicit the honour of standing up with you?'

There could be no way of escaping it—she had no excuses to offer. Richard, last evening, had not troubled himself with making any formal request for the morrow: the way things stood between them, he had no need of doing so. It was tacitly agreed that she would dance with him and with none other. Sir Tristram's return looked to have cast a blight over this happy arrangement in more ways than one. To be summoned so abruptly back to Boswood! To be obliged, moreover, to travel there in the company of one whom at this moment she might heartily have wished at the furthest ends of the earth. Was this to be her last night, and she must waste it on Sir Tristram?

Many a young woman still fresh from the schoolroom, with the smell of chalk still adhering to her person, might have found the solution more readily than Anne: one could always *claim* that one was engaged, even though one was not. Where men are free to choose, whilst women can only wait to be chosen, a little subterfuge must always be necessary if the balance is to stand any chance of being redressed. Anne was not slow to consider it—the thought, indeed, crossed her mind. It was that habitual fault of self-deprecation which made her hesitate. *She* might take it for granted that she should dance only with Richard; but did he? Might it not rather be the case that he would be grateful, for once, for the opportunity of seeking elsewhere for a partner?

She hesitated too long. The moment came—and was gone before she could grasp it. Sir Tristram considered himself as engaged, and duly took his leave; whereupon Isabella, with the air of one whose emotions have been tried beyond all endurance, turned instantly upon Anne with a 'Really! I am quite at a loss to comprehend you! You put me out of all patience! Here have you been, making it as obvious as your wretchedly self-effacing disposition will allow, that all your preference is for Mr Wykeham, and now you would throw away the whole of your last evening upon Sir Tristram! Why in the name of heaven did you not tell him that you were already spoke for?'

Anne took up her discarded netting box.

'I would have done,' she said, 'had I been so. Unfortunately, I am not.'

'Oh! Pooh! Fudge and fiddlesticks! I am very sure that

Mr Wykeham regards you as being so . . . what are you going to tell *him*, pray? If you think he is a young man who can take such sort of disappointment lightly, then I have to tell you that I believe you to be very much mistaken! He is one of those who does not know the meaning of taking things lightly . . . I should not be at all surprised if you were to drive him into doing something desperate, such as challenging Sir Tristram to a duel, when he would very likely be killed, for Sir Tristram is generally reckoned to be an excellent shot and would probably take his head clean off his shoulders . . . then, I suppose, you would be happy!'

She was far from happy when they set out, that evening, for the Rooms. She dreaded lest Richard should arrive after Sir Tristram and she not have the chance to talk with him: she dreaded almost equally what she was to say to him should he arrive *before*.

'There, now!' Isabella rapped smartly upon her companion's arm with her fan. 'He has come early—I knew that he would. I am always right, you see. You would do far better to trust me.'

Anne looked—and saw Richard, making his way towards them in the black satin knee breeches and tail coat which these days he affected, in preference to the gay colours of old.

'Lord!' said Isabella. 'And here is Sir Tristram, almost on top of us from the other direction . . . what a sad mess you have made of everything! You had best go with Sir Tristram and leave Mr Wykeham to me!' She gave Anne a little push. 'Go along! Do as you are told. I know what I am about—which I am inclined to believe is a great deal more than you may be said to do!'

Anne would not have imagined that it was possible, to be at a ball and in such misery. All her thoughts were for Richard—all her *attentions* must be for Sir Tristram. Politeness decreed that she should at least answer his questions. Yes, indeed, she should be excessively sorry to leave Cheltenham! And no, of course she was not attaching any blame to Sir Tristram. She was very sure he had done all that he could in their hehalf. It was most kind in him to be offering them the use of his carriage—and of his protection! Most kind.

'I had hoped that you would find the arrangement agreeable. And you need have no fears on *one* score . . . I will take the precaution, before we set out, of divesting myself of the incriminating bauble!'

'Incrim—oh, yes! Your ring. I had forgot.'

'Forgot? When my very life may be at stake because of it? Miss Fredericks, I am sorely let down! I had hoped you might hold me in higher esteem!'

'It was only a story, after all . . . I am sure you are quite right, and the poor gentleman is motivated by nothing more than his own unfortunate delusions.'

'Hm! So we have abandoned our theory of a broken romance? I am glad at any rate about *that.* I have not the least objection to your feeling sorry for the fellow, but I will confess to pangs of jealousy when you burnish him up like a knight in shining armour!'

Anne smiled; and wished that Sir Tristram might not be quite such an indefatigable talker. Trying to concentrate both upon him and upon her steps, whilst striving at the same time to observe Isabella, was proving a task beyond her capabilities. It could not be done. As she moved further down the set her line of vision became increasingly obscured, until at last she could see nothing but an occasional glimpse of green silk, and that only by turning her head very nearly off her body. Whether Richard was still here—whether he was gone, or standing up with someone else—she had no means of knowing. With every minute that passed, she was in fresh agitation. Never had a set gone on for so long!

It ended at last—but even then Sir Tristram must be with her. Diligently, he escorted her back. Soon, with equal diligence, he would escort her down to tea; and then, with yet more diligence (unless she had recourse to a headache and begged leave to be excused) would lead her out a second time to endure the miseries of yet another set. Anne was beginning to feel the adverse effects of her own faults of character: by an excess of modesty she had made not only herself wretched but all those about her, for she could not suppose that even Sir Tristram was gaining much in the way of satisfaction from the ordeal.

Isabella, when they reached her, was alone, and vigorously fanning herself.

'My dear Sir Tristram! How very glad I am that you are come back! I wonder if you would be so kind as to procure me a glass of lemonade? The atmosphere in this room is positively stifling! I declare my throat is as dry as a piece of old parchment.'

As Sir Tristram, obediently, went off upon his errand, Isabella snapped shut her fan and patted the chair beside her.

'Come and sit down, you ridiculous creature, and stop looking so glum! Did I not tell you to trust me? I have explained everything to him and he has gone away quite happy. If you do not see him again in *Cheltenham*—' she pressed Anne's hand—'I think I may guarantee that it will not be very long before we have the pleasure of his company at *Boswood*.'

CHAPTER FIVE

It was early in the evening, on a warm summer's day at the start of June; and on the terrace of Twelvetrees, in the county of Gloucester, Jack and Fanny Meldrum were enjoying a comfortable chat in the last of the sunshine. They often spent their evenings so, he with his brandy, she with her stitching, talking of this and of that—the children's ailments, the children's achievements, the new drainage scheme for the home meadow—or sometimes not talking of anything at all, but just sitting quietly together in the companionship that proceeds from almost five years of happily married life.

On this particular evening they were engrossed in a subject which came up with perhaps more frequency than any other save only that of the children:

'I suppose,' said Jack, 'that you are thinking of Richard?'

'I find it almost impossible not to.' Fanny, with a sigh, laid down her embroidery. 'Do not you? At such time of year?'

'It crosses my mind, but I refuse to dwell upon it. That has been Richard's failing all these years: too great a preoccupation with what has gone before.'

From the slight pursing of his wife's lips, it would seem that this latter contention was a subject of recurring discussion between them. She said nothing in direct reply, however; but only, after a pause, and taking up her embroidery again: 'It has been almost a twelvemonth now.'

'Mm.'

The grunt with which Jack acknowledged the observation was scarcely one of encouragement. Another pause ensued; then, with an air of defiance: 'He has never left it so long before.'

'He turns up when it pleases him. There is no sense in worrying.'

'There may not be any *sense*—' Fanny stabbed, viciously, with her needle—'but that does not mean I can necessarily cease from doing so! When I think what he is about . . . I dread all the time to hear that some ghastly accident has befallen him, or that he has been taken up on a charge.'

'He knows the risks that he is running. I have told him often enough . . . he will either end up with a bullet through his brain or swinging from Tyburn Tree. If he chooses to expose himself to such dangers, then that is his business. I will not have you fret yourself over him.'

'How can I help it?' Fanny threw down her embroidery once more and turned, accusingly, upon her husband. 'How is it that you can just sit there and seem not to care? When he is your best and oldest friend whom you have known since childhood?'

A muscle twitched in the side of Jack's face.

'It is precisely because he *is* my best and oldest friend that I have given up worrying myself over him . . . the nights that I have lain awake, sweating, wondering what he is up to! The times that I have seen some stranger riding up the drive and have had my heart in my mouth lest it be a messenger come to tell us that the worst has occurred . . . if I had allowed myself the luxury of continuing on that course I should by now be as ripe for the madhouse as he is.'

Fanny bit her lip.

'You cannot really mean that.'

'Mean what? That he is ripe for the madhouse? I most certainly do! He should be taken by force—and chained naked to his bedpost till he comes to his senses—and pray do not look at me in that reproachful fashion! His whole pattern of life since the day that Judith died has been a species of uncontrolled and raving lunacy.'

Fanny dropped her gaze.

'If it has, then I think that it is understandable!

'*Was* understandable . . . five years ago it was understandable.'

Five years ago, his sympathies had been all with Richard. No more than Fanny, nor Richard himself, was he ever likely to blot from his mind the memory of that day, that warm summer day at the start of June, when the tragedy had occurred. He saw it now, as starkly as he ever had—Richard and Judith, cantering ahead—the gig, coming out of nowhere—rounding the corner, bearing straight down upon them . . . A shudder, involuntarily, ran through him, just as it always did, each time that he remembered. He and Fanny, following as usual more sedately behind, had been helpless to do anything but watch in horror as Richard's big black mare, which Judith had insisted upon riding (it had been her proud boast there was no horse she could not handle) had taken fright and gone plunging out of control across the road. The gig, which had never been in control in the first place, had been sent crashing into the ditch, where in the panic of the moment it had been allowed to remain. All immediate attention had been for Judith, lying so horribly still on the hard surface of the road. Only the sudden sound of horse's hooves had alerted them to the fact of the gig's having been extricated from the ditch and got into motion again. Jack could remember, to this day, the pallor on Richard's face as he snatched his pistol from its holster. For just a second he had thought it was his intention to remount and give chase, and had caught at his sleeve in an effort to prevent him—only to find himself sworn at for his pains and roughly flung to one side.

'Damn you! Let me go! Do you wish him to escape?'

He had escaped anyway; but by the narrowest of margins.

The road had been one which had doubled back, quite sharply, upon itself, so that within seconds of taking off the gig had reappeared, with only the width of a small strip of field between itself and them: it had come within easy firing range. The shots that rang out may not have succeeded in their primary objective, but one of them, at least, had found its mark. The following day, Richard had pulled from his pocket a blood-soaked rag, which he had offered Jack for inspection.

'Here! See what you think of this.'

'What is it?'

'Open it up and take a look.'

The Meldrums were a military family. Jack was not accustomed to regard himself as being in any way squeamish. Even he, however, had recoiled at the sight of the grisly object which now lay revealed: part of a severed finger, with the nail still complete upon it and portions of a leather glove still adhering.

'Where in the name of God did you get this?'

'I drove back along the road. It was the one clue that I was able to find.'

'Clue?'

'To Judith's murderer. Whoever he is, he is short of half a finger on his left hand . . . it may not be much to go on, but by Christ I mean to make the most of it! I will get that murdering fiend if it is the last thing I do.'

'Madness!' Jack brought his fist crashing down upon the table at his side. 'Nothing but madness from that day to this!'

'It is a thousand pities,' said Fanny, 'that he cannot meet some pleasant young woman and fall in love with her.'

'Oh! That is your cure for every ill.'

'Yes—and one that has been proven time and again to be effective! If he had someone to care about he would pay rather more attention to the hazards that he runs. Very likely he would give up the whole venture.'

'I should like to think so. Unfortunately, I cannot see it happening. His present life style is hardly conducive to the meeting of pleasant young women, and even if it were he has never been susceptible to the charms of your sex. Other than yourself and Judith, I can think of no female who has ever made even the slightest impression upon him.'

'There was one,' said Fanny, thoughtfully. 'In Cheltenham . . . do you not remember? He danced with her that last evening.'

'Ay! And then raved like a maniac because one week later he was unable to find her again.'

'I have often wondered, if he had succeeded in doing so, whether his life may not have taken a different course.'

'Who knows?' Jack hunched a shoulder. 'Since the question can be none other than hypothetical—'

Sadly, Fanny said: 'I suppose it has become a bit late in the day for speculating.'

'If he is not very careful it will become a bit late in the day for anything at all . . . he has already wasted some of the best years of his life. Do you realise that for the whole of the time we have been married, *he* has been chasing the length and breadth of the land in vain pursuit of what can only be described as an obsession? Five years of fruitless searching! He might as well look for a needle in a haystack for all the chance that he stands.'

'But how can one blame him? When he is doing it for Judith?'

'Doing it for Judith! He is not doing it for Judith, he is doing it because it has become a way of life—because he has lost all sense of where he is headed or why he is headed there. How much longer does he intend to continue? Until he is caught and hanged? The way he is going it will be the gallows' end before he is thirty.' Jack made a noise of disgust. 'And then you would try to tell me that he is sane!'

'Would she, indeed?' An amused voice spoke from the back of the terrace. 'I am glad to know that someone thinks well of me!'

'Richard!' Fanny was out of her chair and into his arms in a trice. 'We have but this second been talking of you!'

'So I gathered—and in no very complimentary fashion, from what I have just heard!'

'Those who eavesdrop,' remarked Jack, upon a yawn, 'must expect to learn a few unpalatable truths about themselves.'

The retort came mockingly: 'Just as those who speak of the devil must expect him to turn up!'

'Oh! We had expected you sooner or later. You should be grateful,' said Jack, rising with an air of ostentatious lethargy to his feet, 'that we still remember you sufficiently to discuss you in any sort of terms at all, considering it is almost a twelve-month since you last deigned to put in an appearance.'

'But last time you saw me you told me I need not trouble to come back until I had mended my ways!'

'And have you?' Breathlessly, Fanny put the question to him. He looked down at her, laughing.

'How can I answer that when it is never specified which ways I must mend?'

Jack shot out an accusing finger.

'You know perfectly well which ways you should mend, and if you have not done so then I am at a loss to know what brings you here! You seem to forget that I am a respectable landowner, and the father of four innocent children.'

Richard pulled a face.

'Then in that case, perhaps, I had better go away again.'

'No!' Fanny wrapped both arms, imploringly, about him. 'Take no notice of what that horrid grumbling creature says. He is only cross because I worry myself over you—and because he does likewise and doesn't care to own to it. We *both* of us worry over you. I cannot tell you how glad I am to see you! And so will the children be, when they wake up and find you here. They are for ever asking after Uncle Richard! You are staying a while, are you not?'

'I am, if I may—if the respectable landowner will permit it.'

'Certainly he will permit it! In any case, he is not as respectable as all that. You would be shocked at some of the things he gets up to.'

'Ay! Smuggling brandy, by the looks of it.' Richard had picked up the flask and was delicately holding it to his nostrils. 'This was never come by by honest means!'

'No, of course it wasn't,' agreed Fanny. 'It arrived quite suddenly in the middle of the night, as quite a few things round here have a tendency to do. I expect when he has finished pretending to sulk he will remember his manners and offer you a glass.'

'Oh! I can help myself—I stand upon no ceremony.'

'So I notice.' Jack spoke drily. 'What brings you here? I trust nothing inopportune?'

Richard grinned.

'Not in the least . . . relax, man! You have naught to fear. There is no one on my tail, and if there were I should certainly not bring them to Twelvetrees.'

'Humph!'

'Have I ever done so?'

'Not as far as I am aware, but there is always a first time.'

'Come! Be fair! I do not abuse friendship in that fashion.'

'No—you limit yourself to abusing it by causing us constant worry and anxiety.' Jack flung himself down again, moodily, into his chair. 'If I had any sense, I would send you packing.'

'You will do no such thing.' Fanny's tone was brisk. 'You will sit there and endeavour to be pleasant whilst I go and arrange for some supper—and while I am away, you will please not to be quarrelling.'

'*I* shall not quarrel.' Richard glanced across, with just a hint of challenge, at Jack. 'Unless you mean to push me to it?'

'Push you to it! Of course I do not mean to push you to it. It is just that you try me beyond all endurance! My relief when I know you to be safe is so immoderate that I grow infuriated at myself. Why I should continue to care is quite beyond me to imagine. But damn your eyes, I do care! And, indeed—' Jack leaned forward and gripped Richard's hand—'I am mighty happy to see you.'

'And I you—for all your curmudgeonly ways. It may surprise you to know that I am actually quite fond of you.'

'Then why in the name of God do you not come more often?'

'Possibly because I am not quite such an insensitive clod as you would make me out to be . . . I am very well aware of your position.'

'Tush, man! What is position?'

'Something not to be sneered at, when you have a wife and children to consider. If it ever became known that you were consorting with—' he waved a hand—'a common highwayman—'

'You are not a common highwayman but a damned quixotic fool who seems not to know when enough is enough! When do you mean to give up this tomfoolery and start leading a normal life again?'

'Perhaps rather sooner than you had imagined.'

'What?' Jack sat back, bolt upright, on his chair. 'You would have me believe that you are seriously considering—'

'Seriously considering a return to normality . . . yes. I had hoped that it would please you.'

'Please me? It gladdens me more than I can possibly say!'

'Mind, I make no promises. It all depends . . . upon what transpires during the time that I am here.'

'Oh?'

'I have—acquaintances—not a million miles away. They live just outside Oxford. A place called Boswood. It is possible you may have heard of them—the name is Fredericks.'

'Fredericks? No; I don't seem to—wait! Fredericks . . . was that not the name of the young woman you met in Cheltenham? The young woman you danced with—'

He stopped himself, just in time, the words "that last night" frozen on his lips. Richard, however, appeared to notice nothing amiss. He nodded, amiably.

'The young woman I danced with. Precisely. I had thought that you would remember.'

'And she is the one who lives near Oxford?'

'Just so.'

A smile slowly spread itself across Jack's face.

'I suppose I need hardly ask whether the young lady is married?'

'As at this moment, she remains Miss Fredericks. I hope to persuade her into doing something to alter the situation in the very near future.'

'Well! For once you have my most hearty approval . . . this is splendid news! Do I have your permission to tell Fanny?

She will be overjoyed to hear it—she is a quite incurable romantic. She has been lecturing me only this evening on the subject.'

'What subject is that?' Fanny had reappeared on the terrace. 'What is it that I have been lecturing you on?'

'Why—' Jack swung round, laughing. 'On the ability of love to redeem even the deepest dyed villain . . . and the need of a certain young gentleman of our acquaintance to be finding himself an agreeable female that he may lose his heart to!'

Fanny blushed.

'Oh! That! But I was only speaking in general, you know. I meant nothing personal by it.'

'Did you not? Well! That is a pity, when here he has gone and done the very thing that you were advocating . . . he has not only found himself an agreeable female but is actually proposing, if she will have him, to make an honest woman of her.'

'Richard!' Fanny spun round, her eyes shining. 'Oh, Richard! I am so very, very happy for you!

He smiled.

'You had better postpone your congratulations until I know whether she will have me.'

'Of course she will have you!' Fanny sounded indignant. 'Why should she not?'

'I am sure that Jack could supply you with a dozen good reasons why she should not!'

'Well, but naturally you will not tell her—' Fanny broke off, in confusion. 'That is—I mean—she does not have to know—'

'What I have been up to these past few years?'

'I think it would be a very great mistake,' said Fanny, earnestly, 'if you were to mention anything of it. It is, after all, quite unnecessary, for now that you are in love you will obviously be adopting a totally different style of life.' She looked up at him, rather anxiously. 'Will you not?'

'Yes; he will,' said Jack. 'He has already given me his word on it.'

'Well! There you are, then! There is no problem. Dear Richard!' Fanny tucked her hand, companionably, into his.

'I am so very glad that you have found someone! Is she anybody one might know?'

'Very possibly. Her name is Miss Fredericks.'

'Fredericks! That is the girl you danced with, in Cheltenham—I remember her perfectly! She was fair, and very dainty.'

'And is so still. *She* has changed not one jot.'

'No more have you,' said Fanny, loyally.

'I am afraid that is not quite true, but at least she recognised me and remembered who I was—I counted that as some kind of victory. At any rate, it gave me the courage to continue. Had she simply looked straight through me, I believe I should have been sufficiently the coward to have turned tail and slunk out.'

'No girl who has any sense,' said Fanny, warmly, 'would *ever* look straight through you. But how came you to meet her again, after all this time?'

Richard hesitated.

'Officially, I—I rediscovered her, as you might say, in the Assembly Rooms at Cheltenham.'

'Oh?' Jack raised an eyebrow. 'And unofficially? As you might say?'

'Unofficially, I—er—held up her carriage on the Oxford road . . .'

'So what do you think?' said Jack, as later that evening he and Fanny were once again alone together.

'I think—' Fanny smiled, complacently, at her reflection in the glass—'I think it is the very best thing that could ever have happened. It is precisely the very thing that he has needed.'

'I only hope to heaven it works out. If anything were to go wrong—'

'What could?' Fanny turned, with a frown. '*He* is not going to tell Miss Fredericks of his past activities, and I am sure that neither you nor I will ever breathe a word of it.'

'Obviously not.'

'Then what is it that bothers you?'

'I am not quite sure, except . . . except that I tremble for his future if this girl should turn him down.'

'She will not turn him down.' Fanny dismissed the idea, scornfully. 'He is heir to a small fortune, and has a pretty face to go with it. What girl in her right mind, unless she were the daughter of a duke, or some such grand thing, would ever dream of *turning him down*? Not only that—' she picked up her hair brush and began, determinedly, to beat at her hair with it—'not only that, he has great charm of manner and an exceedingly fetching way of smiling at one . . . if I had not been foolish enough to fall in love with his horrid great cart horse of a friend, I should be in grave danger of swooning over him myself.'

'I have been meaning for some time—' in the privacy of their bedroom, only a few miles away, at Boswood, in the neighbouring county of Oxford, Adam Fredericks put the question to his wife—'I have been meaning for some time to ask you, what your opinion is of Sir Tristram?'

'Sir Tristram?' Isabella paused, thoughtfully, in her nightly task of rubbing cream into her cheeks. 'I find him perfectly agreeable. I would not place him on a pedestal, but I have nothing against him.'

'And Anne? Does *she* find him agreeable?'

'She has certainly never said anything to the contrary.'

'So she would not consider it distateful if he were to make her an offer of marriage?'

'Oh! So that is it.' Isabella resumed her rubbing. 'Does he intend to do so?'

'He intimated as such, last time that he was here.'

'Then I am afraid that he will be in for a disappointment: she will not have him.'

'What!' Adam looked thunderstruck. 'What do you mean, she will not have him?'

'I mean that she will not have him . . . if he had only sought my advice first, I might have spared him the mortification. I always think,' said Isabella, 'that it must be exceedingly uncomfortable for a gentleman to have his suit refused. It is greatly to be regretted that he did not come to me . . . I might then have broke it to him, gently, that he stood no chance.'

'I see.' Adam's face was grim. 'Are you trying to tell me that there is someone else?'

'Someone whom she is fallen head over heels in love with. Wild horses would not drag it from her, but she betrays herself at every turn . . . you would smile to see the way her eyes light up, whenever he comes anywhere near!'

Just at that moment, Adam did not look as though he should be much inclined to smile at anything at all: his expression was rather one of displeasure than of delight. Isabella, taking note, hurried on.

'I should have told you sooner. I had meant to do so, only somehow or other the opportunity did not arise, and I had not the least idea that Sir Tristram—well, I knew, of course, that he was interested—he made *that* quite plain—but the fact is, in any case, that it is all to be kept a secret—from Anne, that is. You must on no account mention anything of it to her! You must give me your word. It is to be a surprise, on her birthday—we have arranged it all between us. The young man is gone to stay with friends in Gloucester and is to ride over to Boswood during the morning. You will then be able to meet him, and satisfy yourself as to his respectability, and if he does not put the question to her that same day then I shall never trust my own judgement again!'

Still, Adam did not smile.

'I swear it,' said Isabella. 'I never shall!'

'It is not up to you to be trusting your own judgement.' The words came out coldly. 'In matters pertaining to my sister, it is up to me to decide who is fit to make her a proposal and who is not.'

'Well—yes! Of course! I had not meant to usurp your authority. That is why I said, that you would be able to meet him and satisfy yourself as to his respectability.'

'You had no right to be inviting him here. No right at all!' Adam's face, in the moonlight, had grown very pale. 'You ought never to have encouraged him. It was wrong of you. Exceedingly wrong!'

'But—' Isabella faltered, taken aback by this most uncharacteristic outburst. Her husband's temper might be gloomy, but it was not as a rule harsh. 'I am sorry,' she said, 'if I have displeased you, but I am sure that once you have met the young man—'

'I have no need of meeting him! I prefer that he does not come here.'

Isabella's eyebrows went up, in spite of herself.

'How can you say so? When you have not the least idea of what he is like! I have not even told you his name.'

'I already know his name. Sir Tristram told me.'

'Sir *Tristram?* And what, pray, has it to do with him?'

'I asked him how you went on. He could hardly have answered me honestly had he failed to inform me of the sort of company that my sister was keeping.'

'If he has said anything against Mr Wykeham, you may set it down to simple jealousy! I see now why you brought us back so speedily . . . Sir Tristram has been filling your head with scurrilous tales—scheming and contriving to have us taken out of harm's way, so that the field might be left clear for *him*. And there we were, thinking that he was working *for* us . . . I never heard of anything so shabby!'

'There is nothing shabby about it. He had Anne's best interests at heart.'

'If you will believe *that*,' said Isabella, 'you will believe anything.'

'I suppose you do not doubt that *I* have her best interests at heart?'

'Not for a moment. But I am very sure that Sir Tristram—'

'Never mind Sir Tristram! When you spoke just now of having Anne taken out of harm's way, you were nearer the truth than you realised . . . would you have her ally herself to one whose sanity is in question?'

'Mr Wykeham's sanity is no more in question than yours or mine! That is precisely what I mean about scurrilous tales. Just because he had the misfortune, five years ago, to lose a sister, and to suffer all the grief that anyone of any sensibility must necessarily feel at such a melancholy occurrence—'

'I think,' said Adam, 'that you would do well to stop at that point.'

'Stop? Why should I stop? Such tales rouse my indignation!'

'Then perhaps I had better remind you that Mr Wykeham is not the only person in this world to have endured misfortune . . . *I* had the misfortune to lose both my parents, and very nearly my sister, as well. I suffered just as much grief as might have been expected: I did not have to be locked up in a madhouse for my own protection.'

Isabella started, and grew red.

'That is only a rumour.'

'Even rumours do not proceed from no cause. Have you ever tried asking him, where he has been these past few years? I think if you did, you would receive no very coherant reply.'

There was a silence. Isabella, plainly shaken, stared and said nothing.

'You were not to know,' said Adam, 'though had you seen fit to consult me I might have alerted you.'

She swallowed.

'I had thought the connexion unexceptionable—she knew him from when she was there before. He seems so—so very gentlemanlike.'

'I am certain that he is so! You would hardly have allowed her to renew the acquaintance had such not been the case. Do not misread me: I have nothing against his *social* standing. It is this other business which gives cause for alarm.'

Isabella looked up at him, pleadingly.

'Can we really be so sure that it is not simply a case of malicious gossip?'

'If you are harking back to Sir Tristram—'

'No! Not just Sir Tristram! *Him* I can dismiss—'

She stopped; too late.

'You mean,' said Adam, 'that there have been others?'

Her silence gave its own reply.

'And then you ask me whether we can be sure?' Adam shook his head. 'You know as well as I that there is never any smoke without a fire . . . you have answered your own question.'

'Yes—' The word came out reluctantly.

'You see that it is true.'

'Yes—'

'You must not blame yourself! You acted as you thought best. I had no right to speak sharply to you—your only fault lay in not consulting me. Pray, now, don't weep! I hate to think that I have upset you.'

Through her tears, in muffled tones, Isabella could be heard to declare that it was not for herself that she was upset, but for "poor Mr Wykeham".

'Not knowing that we know—that people talk of him behind his back—'

'Yes. Well—' Adam straightened up. 'It is very sad for him, I do not doubt, but it is Anne we must be thinking of. All our duty is towards *her*. Where there is any taint—even the least hint or suspicion—it plainly behoves us to proceed with caution. In this case, I fear, there is quite considerable taint and a great deal more than mere *suspicion:* there is virtual certainty. The whole of the family is unstable—the girl herself was so. Totally uncontrollable. That is how she came to get herself killed. I would not wish' (as Isabella opened her mouth) 'to appear unsympathetic, but no young woman who was not reckless to a degree bordering on insanity would attempt the riding of a horse so patently beyond her ability to handle—and no brother who was not morally, I would even say *criminally*, blind to his fraternal duties would ever dream of allowing her to do so. In that sense, he has only himself to blame. That does not mean, of course, that one does not feel for him; only that one must not lose sight of where one's primary obligations lie. Anne is our chief care. *She* must be the one to be safeguarded.'

'But—' Isabella hiccuped, and groped for a handkerchief. 'What are we to tell her?'

'It will probably be best if we tell her nothing at all. It is unfortunate that matters have been allowed to progress so far, but as against that there is the lucky chance of your having kept this prospective visit a secret from her. If she knows nothing of it, she cannot be disappointed when it fails to come off.'

'But I—' Isabella dabbed, despairingly, at her eyes—'I don't see how we are to stop it.'

'That is easily done. You will write to the young man and

explain that our circumstances have changed and that the visit is no longer possible.'

'I can't! I told you . . . he is staying with friends. I don't know their direction or anything ab-bout them. He will just have to c-come and you will have to break it to him yourself.'

Adam stood a moment, gnawing at his lower lip.

'You s-see?' Isabella tipped her head back, in an effort to stem the flood of her tears. 'When it comes to the point you like to do it n-no more than I.'

'I do not pretend to *like* to do it—it is not something that can be shirked, however. Will Anne wish to be visiting Miss Morcomb on her birthday morning? Or will she rather drive into Oxford to make some purchases? I am sure you can arrange for one or the other.'

Isabella gazed at him, doubtfully.

'You would rather we were not here?'

'I think it would be advisable. If she were to catch sight of him from a window—'

Fresh tears started to Isabella's eyes.

'I wish there were some other way! It is cruel, to deceive her so!'

'It would be even more cruel to stand by and do nothing. Imagine how you would feel if—'

'Yes! Yes! Pray do not continue, I cannot bear it! When I think of Anne—of poor Mr Wykeham—oh, Adam!' She clutched, beseechingly, at her husband's arm. 'You will be nice to him? You will break it as kindly as possible?'

Gravely, he loosened her grip on the material of his coat.

'I will do what has to be done. Remember . . . I am only thinking of Anne.'

CHAPTER SIX

'My!' said Jack. 'We are looking very handsome!'

'Thank you kindly, sir.' Richard grinned, inclining his head in acknowledgement of the compliment. 'Such was the intention.'

'Then the intention can only be said to have succeeded . . . but why the buckskins, might I ask? You are surely not intending to ride there?'

'Certainly I am going to ride there! Why should I not? The sun is out, the sky is clear—'

'And since when has it been the custom that a gentleman presents himself for a lady's approval wearing riding breeches and top boots?'

'Oh! Anne will not mind. We don't stand upon ceremony.'

'You mean that she has to put up with the same cavalier treatment as I am forced to tolerate . . . why do you not take the carriage? It will be far more fitting.'

'Very likely, but I cannot endure to be shut in. Besides,

I should be terrified the whole way lest some maniac with a pistol held us up!'

'Your fears would be quite groundless: there is only one maniac with a pistol in these parts, so far as I am aware.—If you do not like to be shut in, then take the gig and drive yourself.'

'I would, but you see—' Richard smiled, disarmingly—'it is so long since I have handled the ribbons that I have quite forgot the art of it.'

'Rubbish! That is the paltriest excuse I ever heard. Why are you so set on going there by horseback?'

'It is not so much that I am set on it as that it has become a habit. Pathetic though it may seem, I no longer feel comfortable using any other mode of transport.'

'Then I would suggest the time has come for you to start accustoming yourself! You will hardly expect Miss Fredericks to go everywhere with you on the top of a horse.'

'So soon as she has signified her assent to become Mrs Wykeham, I give you my word, I will set up my own carriage and drive about the country as sedate as you please. For the moment, you must be patient and indulge me.'

'When do I ever not?' Jack pulled a wry face. 'I begin to think I have been patient for far too long. You take advantage of my good nature.'

'Ah, Jack! Have a heart! To-morrow you may be as cross with me as you like. But for to-day, at least, let me feel that I have you on my side.'

'Well, of course you do, you damned fool! You don't need me to tell you that. Go on! Be off with you! The sooner you go, the sooner you will be back.' And the sooner, he added, watching Richard stride off in the direction of the stables, shall I be able to rest easy in my bed at nights . . .

From the moment of waking, Anne had been faced with the sobering truth that she was now, in good earnest, four and twenty years of age. No more "approaching"—no more "almost": she was *there*. It was not, perhaps, such a very great age as ages go—the world, after all, was full of people far older; but still, there could be no denying that it was a twelve months further on from twenty-three. At twenty-three one might still, with some justification, be described as a young girl: at twenty-four, one had forfeited all right.

It did not do to dwell on it, and in normal circumstances she would not have done so. Circumstances, however, were *not* normal. She had been back to Cheltenham and nothing could ever again be the same as it had been. For better or for worse, the Anne Fredericks who had left Boswood at the beginning of May was not the Anne Fredericks who had returned at the end of it. She had recaptured the sensation of being romantically in love and optimistic for the future: it was difficult to be reconciled to the fact of being four and twenty years of age and only one year off being twenty-five.

If Richard would only come, she felt that perhaps she should not mind it so very much, but almost a week had passed since they had been called back to Boswood and still there was no sign of him. This morning, as every morning, she sustained herself with the thought that here was a new day, with its full complement of hours, in which anything might happen; so that when Isabella, at breakfast, brightly suggested a trip into Oxford to "gaze at the shops and maybe make some purchases", she was in some doubts as to whether she really wished to be absenting herself for as long as such a trip would entail. If Richard were to call, and she not be there—

'I think that you should go,' said Adam. 'A drive in the fresh air will do you a world of good.'

'And besides,' said Isabella, 'I have been most particularly wishing to buy some new trimmings for that bonnet I got whilst we were in Cheltenham. I thought at the time that it was a mistake—that fly-away style does not in the least become me.'

'I think it becomes you very well,' said Anne.

'Oh, no! You are quite wrong. I have not the face for it. My idea is to purchase a length of something pretty and see what may be done in the way of refashioning.'

'You will ruin it if you try that.'

'Not if I have you to help me.' Isabella looked at her, coaxingly. 'You are always so clever at that kind of thing.'

Anne laughed.

'Flattery will avail you nothing! I hate to spoil a good bonnet.'

'Then you shall have it for yourself and we shall go into Oxford and buy me another.'

'That will be a very expensive way of refashioning!'

'Oh! I am past caring for the expense . . . I have come to hate the thing so much I had as soon cut it into pieces as put it on my head again.'

'Well! If that is the way you feel—'

'You had better go,' said Adam. 'It will be best if you do.'

'And on our way back,' said Isabella, 'we may make a détour and call in upon Miss Morcomb . . . if we set out immediately after breakfast, you know, we may easily be home again in time for dinner.'

Boswood House was a spacious, red-brick dwelling, built in the Jacobean style and approached by an imposing avenue of flowering chestnuts. The landscaped park which enclosed it was not extensive, but was nonetheless very prettily laid out, with a lake bordered by weeping willows, and formal gardens with flower beds as one drew close to the house. A few years back, the young buck that had been Richard Wykeham would have looked upon it with scorn as being too neat—too orderly—too soft and southern for his more rugged taste. Now, he thought of it purely as a setting for Anne; and in that context found it perfect. To be sure, it lacked the sheer vast expanse of the family acres up in Yorkshire, but Anne was not one who could bloom in a vast expanse. Her gentle manners would be crushed by the harshness of rugged desolation: she needed the softness of grass and of trees, as she had here at Boswood. When they were married, he thought, he would find her somewhere similar. She would doubtless like to be near her brother, and when once she had met Jack and Fanny he had every confidence in her wishing to be near them, as well. In any case, there could be no question of a return to Yorkshire. His mama might secretly wish for it—indeed, he was very sure that she did—but it was not up to her. So long as his *father*—

His jaw tightened. He would not think of his father. Thinking of his father made him think of Judith, and that was something he must start learning not to do. *Anne*, now, must be his first concern.

He tethered the mare and walked up the shallow flight of steps leading to the house. There was some kind of trailing thing, with delicate rose-pink leaves, growing over the front door and all across the wall. He looked at it, approvingly. He and Anne would have a house with a trailing thing. Up in Yorkshire, the walls were cold and bare, with nothing growing upon them save the occasional piece of moss. Anne would not care for Yorkshire. Even in the event of a reconciliation—and *he* would be prepared, in spite of the harsh words that had been spoken—he would not ask her to live up there. She belonged in milder climes: he would not uproot her.

The front door had opened. —He stepped forward.

'If you would tell the lady of the house that Mr Wykeham is here—I regret I have no card, but I believe you will find that I am expected.'

'I beg your pardon, sir.' The man made no move either to relieve him of his hat and gloves or to stand to one side and allow him in. 'Mrs Fredericks is gone into Oxford with Miss Anne.'

'Oh! Well, perhaps I am a little in advance. At what hour do you expect them back?'

'Not until later in the afternoon, sir. Mrs Fredericks mentioned it particularly, that they should be back in time for dinner.'

'Which is when?'

'Mrs Fredericks commonly orders it for three o'clock, sir, when the family is alone.'

'And to-day?'

'There is no one expected, sir, so far as I am aware.'

'Tut!' Richard clicked his tongue, impatiently. 'Here is some stupid mistake on my part! I have obviously got my days mixed. Oblige me by setting me right and telling me whether this is or is not a Thursday, and whether it is or is not the 6th June?'

'My understanding is that it is both, sir!'

'And it is also your understanding that it is Miss Frederick's birthday?'

'It is indeed, sir.'

'Then I am at a loss to know where I have gone wrong. Is *Mr* Fredericks by any chance at home, or is he, too, not expected back until later in the afternoon?'

'Mr Fredericks, as I believe, is in the library, sir.'

'Then perhaps you would be good enough to inform him that I am here.'

'Very good, sir. If I might just inquire again what the name was?'

Richard raised an eyebrow. Mildly, he said: 'The name is Wykeham.'

'Yes, sir. If you would care to step inside—'

'Are you quite sure that you would not prefer me to remain upon the doorstep?'

'I will tell Mr Fredericks that you are here, sir.'

The man withdrew. Richard, left to kick his heels in the hall, tossed hat and gloves upon a nearby chair and stared moodily up at a painting of some monstrous ugly female in a yellow wig that hung upon the opposite wall. It was hard—very hard—to escape the conclusion that he was being deliberately snubbed. He could think of no reason why he should be, unless by some ghastly mischance—but that was not possible! Other than Jack and Fanny, no one had the least cause for suspicion regarding his activities over the past few years. His secret, he knew, was quite safe with *them*.

The only other possibility that presented itself was too hideous to be thought of. The idea that *Anne*—but, then, if she had not recognised him at the time, it was hardly very likely, was it, that she would suddenly make the connexion all these weeks afterwards? No! Of course it was not. What was far *more* likely was that the arrangements that had been agreed upon had simply slipped the memory of that bird-brained sister-in-law of hers. He should not be at all surprised. Words tumbled out of her mouth so fast, the chances were she forgot them the very minute they had been uttered. That would be what it was. *She* had forgotten, and Anne had never known—and he himself was behaving like some over-sensitive schoolboy, imagining slights where none was intended. He would speak to the brother, and they would speedily have things settled.

He turned, at the sound of a footfall behind him: the manservant had reappeared.

'I informed Mr Fredericks that you were here, sir. He asked me to convey his most sincere apologies for any inconvenience that may have been caused.'

Did he so? Well! That was mighty civil of him . . . considering, thought Richard, that I have just rode the better part of ten miles to come here.

'Mr Fredericks did wonder, sir, whether perhaps there might not have been some error—'

'Error! There has indeed. There is no *perhaps* about it.'

'—in the matter of names, sir. He suggested that possibly you may have misheard Fredericks for something else?'

Ay! For Smith or Montmorency, no doubt—and Boswood House for Castle Howard. Richard said coldly: 'I should like to be allowed to speak to Mr Fredericks, if you please. I shall be obliged if you will take me to him straight away.'

The man's face remained impassive.

'Mr Fredericks very much regrets, sir, but he cannot be disturbed just at this moment. He asked me sir, to give you this—'

Richard took the folded sheet of paper that was being held out to him. His expression grew grim as he read the few terse lines scrawled therein:

I do not care for unpleasantness. I shall be greatly obliged if you will leave my premises forthwith and make no further attempt at communication with my sister.—I believe I have no need of spelling out my reasons for not wishing the acquaintance to continue.

No; no need at all. White-faced, Richard turned. He snatched up his hat and gloves.

The manservant hastened forward to open the door.

'Will there be any message, sir?'

'No.' Richard spoke curtly. 'No message.'

Where would be the point? Anne had quite obviously

made the connexion—quite obviously passed on the information to her brother. She was not very likely to care—*now*—whether he called or whether he did not. It would probably be less of an embarrassment to her if she were left in ignorance. She plainly had no desire to see him again: she had made *that* obvious enough. Had she been willing to give him the benefit of the doubt, she would have stayed her hand until she had had a chance to tackle him on the subject and to hear his explanations. A sense of bitterness pervaded him: she was not interested in hearing his explanations. She preferred to set him down as a common criminal without even giving him the opportunity to speak in his own defence. Very well, then! He swung himself up into the saddle. If that was how little she thought of him—

He rode back along the avenue of flowering chestnuts, past the formal gardens and the lake with its border of willows. As he left the park behind him, the land dipped down, into the vale of a wooded hill. He could see the road winding ahead, amongst the trees, and a single carriage in the distance, making its way towards him. Instinctively, he reined in, reaching up a hand for the scarf which he kept knotted about his neck for just such occasions. It was an act prompted by sheer force of habit: the scarf was not there. He had not set out that morning with the intention of holding up any carriages. He had been going, had he not, to make a proposal of marriage? No matter! A neckcloth would serve the same purpose. Grimly, he wrenched it undone, pulling the mare, as he did so, into the shelter of the trees. He had given his word to Jack, but that word had been conditional. He was no longer bound by it. Since Anne would not have him—

The carriage was approaching rapidly. It was drawn by a pair of strong looking bays, and was making good speed even up the slope of the hill. If the thing were to be done, then let it be done now. Another moment, and the opportunity would be gone.

Determinedly, he took his pistol from its holster and spurred the mare forward. Since Anne would not have him, he might gamble his life as he chose. What did he care for the gallows' end? Tyburn Tree held no terrors for him. He should just as soon end up swinging by the neck at the age of thirty as go creeping lamely on towards his dotage. Jack might die quietly in his bed if he would: he was damned if he was going to submit so tamely.

Oxford had been visited, the shops duly gazed at, the new bonnet purchased; Miss Morcomb had been taken in upon the way home and expressed delight in Anne's improved looks.

'I have scarcely ever seen you so blooming! There must be something in the air of Cheltenham' (this with a wink and a nod and an arch smile in Isabella's direction) 'that agrees with you more than commonly . . .'

They arrived back at Boswood, as planned, with just sufficient time to wash and make a change of dress before sitting down to dine. As Anne descended the stairs, wearing a gown of yellow crêpe which did not particularly flatter her, but which had happened to be the first thing which came to hand, Adam emerged from the drawing room and seeing her there stepped quickly across.

'I am glad you are back punctually. We have an unexpected visitor.'

'Oh?' Her heart leapt. He had come—and on her birthday! Was ever such happy coincidence? She put up a hand, somewhat anxiously, to her hair. Had she brushed it? She could not remember!

'I could scarcely do otherwise—' Adam sounded apologetic—'than ask him to stay and take dinner with us. I hope it will not tax you too much?'

'Tax me? Not in the slightest! I love to have visitors. My only regret is that I did not know sooner. I might then—' she pulled a rueful face—'have taken rather more care with my appearance.'

'You are not satisfied with the way you look? You would like to make some change? Then why do you not do so? I am sure Sir Tristram will not mind giving you a few extra minutes.'

'Sir—' The blood drained from her cheeks. For just a moment, she thought she might almost be going to faint. 'Sir Tristram?' she whispered.

'Yes. He is come all the way over from Tewkesbury. I could hardly send him away again. Indeed, I have offered him a bed for the night. It seemed the—' He broke off. 'What is amiss? You are suddenly looking pale! Are you unwell?'

She forced herself to swallow.

'No! Not at all.'

'Are you quite certain?'

Adam placed a hand beneath her elbow. He seemed uneasy. Flustered—almost nervous. She reminded herself, with an effort, that visitors of any kind were an ordeal to him; visitors who turned up without warning, even more so. *She* must not be the one to go to pieces.

'I assure you, I am perfectly all right . . . it is just that I was not expecting anyone to be here, and female vanity does prefer a little notice of such things!'

'If you wish to go back upstairs and make some adjustments in your dress, I can always present your excuses.'

'Please don't. It is not worth disrupting everyone.' Not for Sir Tristram. Had it been *Richard*—

'But I want you to be comfortable!' Adam was starting to grow agitated. 'I want you to be happy . . . you will not be so if you are worried all the time about your appearance. Let me arrange for dinner to be put back by half an hour.'

'Certainly not! I never heard of such a thing! I should hope I am not so vain as all that.'

'There is nothing vain about it. On the contrary, it is quite right and proper. A young woman must be exceedingly odd if she does not wish to look her best in front of—'

'In front of what?' Isabella had now joined them. 'Why are you having private conversations on the stairs? In front of what must it be exceedingly odd if one does not wish to look one's best?'

'In front of company,' said Adam.

'Company?' Isabella appeared startled. 'What company is this?'

'Sir Tristram is here,' said Anne.

'Oh! Sir Tristram! That is all right. *He* is almost become one of the family.'

'Anne would still wish to look her best,' insisted Adam.

'Well—yes.' Isabella regarded her sister-in-law, critically. 'It has to be said that that gown is not one of your *most* becoming.'

'But, however, it will have to do.' Anne had recovered her composure, and with it a measure of defiance. The yellow gown would serve very well. She did not care for Sir Tristram: the last thing she wished was to be encouraging him. 'One cannot have dinner put back only so that I may spend half an hour re-arranging myself. Cook would be in a fury, and quite rightly so.'

'It is nothing to do with Cook! If you are unhappy with your looks—'

'I do not care tuppence for my looks!' Of what importance were her looks, since Richard was not here to be affected by them? 'I wish only to be left alone to remain as I am. Why do we not go in?'

Adam and Isabella exchanged glances. Isabella gave a slight, warning shake of the head. Displays of irritation coming from Anne were a rarity. The message, quite clearly, was intended to convey: *It will be better if you do not push her*. Thankfully, Adam heeded the advice. The issue was dropped, Anne was allowed to remain as she was. Even with this dispensation, she found it difficult to sustain any degree of liveliness. There was a want of animation, a general depression of spirit, which could not but be remarked.—Sir Tristram, being Sir Tristram, duly remarked it.

'Miss Fredericks is very silent! Does she sit in judgement on us?'

'I sit in judgement upon nobody,' said Anne.

'But yet our poor attempts at conversation would seem to rouse no sparks in you.'

'I take it all in.'

'But you do not respond! You are usually one of the first to rally me and set me right when I go wrong.'

'Perhaps to-day I am not in the mood for rallying. I am happy just to listen.'

'But I am not happy just to be listened to! Would you have me perform a monologue? How boring I should be! I need your comments to spice my talk and give it a little flavour.'

Anne bent her head; she had never felt less inclined for banter. Adam, with a gallant attempt at coming to her rescue, said: 'Anne has always had a tendency to quietness. She is not much of a one for lively prattle.'

'There I must beg to disagree! When she was in Cheltenham she was as avid a conversationalist as ever I have met. We enjoyed many a spirited exchange of views—did we not, Miss Fredericks?'

'I think perhaps when she was in Cheltenham,' said Adam, gravely, 'she was exposed to rather more in the way of excitement than was strictly good for her. She is used to lead a very quiet life here at Boswood.'

'Yes,' said Isabella. 'It is a somewhat retiring sort of place.'

'I cannot comment—' Sir Tristram spoke after a moment's pause for reflection—'on its being retiring, but one thing I know, and that is that it certainly cannot be described as *uneventful* . . . not, at any rate, if my experience of this morning is anything to go by.'

'Oh?' Isabella raised both eyebrows. 'You have had an *experience?* Here at *Bos*wood?'

'I have had an experience indeed—and practically upon your very doorstep. I have been in two minds whether or not to mention it, but if there is one subject guaranteed to rouse Miss Fredericks' interest it is this, for it was just such an occurrence as she herself has warned me of.—There!' (as Anne looked up, in spite of herself) 'I knew she would not be able to resist! You are wondering, are you not, what in the wide world I can be talking about? Confess it! You are curious! Let me give you a clue . . . if I tell you that I had neglected to take the precaution of removing the *bauble*—' he held up his left hand, on one finger of which glinted his heavy silver signet ring—'but that nonetheless I emerged unscathed—'

'Emerged unscathed?' Isabella's eyes grew gratifyingly round. 'Anne, enlighten us! *You* are in on the secret . . . what is Sir Tristram talking of?'

'I collect,' said Anne, 'that what he is talking of is an experience which is most particularly common in the environs of Cheltenham.'

'And what, pray, is *that* supposed to mean?'

'I think it must mean that he was held up in his carriage.'

'Precisely! And within scarcely a mile of Boswood itself. It would seem the gentleman is growing bold . . . he is no longer confining himself to the environs of Cheltenham, but has taken to roaming further afield.'

'He stopped you?' The question came, hoarsely, from Adam.

'He stopped me,' said Sir Tristram.

'And you—'

'Oh, I objected! You may be very sure of that.' Sir Tristram reached out a hand for his wine glass. 'I flatter myself I am somewhat faster on the draw than most. At any rate, I have given him something to remember me by . . . he will not hold up my carriage again in a hurry!'

'So long as you have not killed him,' said Isabella. 'I should not like to think you had done that.'

'Why not?' Adam turned on her, harshly. 'Why should he not exercise his rights? The man is nothing but a common felon. If the law ever caught up with him, they would show him no mercy. Why should his victims be expected to do so?'

'Well, naturally, if one is frightened,' said Isabella, 'there is no telling how one may react. I am sure nobody could be *blamed* for killing him, I am only saying that it would be a very great shame if they did.'

'*Shame?*' Adam sounded as if he could not believe his ears. 'To shoot a common *highwayman?*'

'Oh, but he is not! That is what I am saying . . . he never actually takes anything, you know, nor does anyone any harm. Only holds up their carriages and then apologises for inconveniencing them.'

'And you call that not doing any harm? Suppose the carriage were to contain an old gentleman with a weak heart? Or a lady in a delicate condition?'

'Certainly,' agreed Isabella, 'it would be better if he did *not* go about holding people up in the way that he does. I am not defending it. It is very wrong of him, and there can be no justification for such behaviour. But as against that, one must be charitable. The poor young man really cannot help himself. I do very much hope—' she turned, earnestly, to Sir Tristram—'that you did him no serious harm?'

'I put a bullet through his ribs for him.—I doubt he will die of it.'

'It is a thousand pities,' muttered Adam, 'that you didn't put it through his heart.'

'Come, now!' Sir Tristram seemed amused. 'You could hardly expect me to do that . . . when the poor young man cannot help himself? It would be most unsportsmanlike! Besides, it would make me unpopular with the ladies. You must know—' he smiled, in Anne's direction—'that Miss Fredericks in particular cherishes a soft spot for this misguided young gentleman. She has a theory that at some stage in the past he has been done a grievous wrong and is out to discover the miscreant and bring him to book.'

'I have not heard this!' said Isabella. 'I was under the impression that he had suffered a disappointment in love?'

'Oh, no! You are all behind the times. That is a theory which has been discredited. Miss Fredericks now prefers something rather more Gothic.—Do you not, Miss Fredericks?'

'I am sure I don't prefer anything at all,' said Anne. 'I cannot understand why you should have found the need to be taking shots at him, when you know as well as anyone that he is perfectly harmless—'

'Ah! But is he? When I am wearing The Bauble? That is the question, is it not?'

If it were, then Anne ignored it.

'I can only say that I am exceedingly thankful you chose not to kill him. I daresay you might have done so, had you really wished, for I have heard that you are an excellent shot. As far as I am concerned, therefore, the fact that you spared him can only be to your credit.'

'Well!' Sir Tristram directed a sly glance across the table at Adam. 'It seems that I have done *some*thing right!'

CHAPTER SEVEN

'It grows dark,' said Jack.

'You want more light?' Fanny looked up from the slippers she was embroidering. 'Why do you not ring for Porson and ask him to bring another branch of candles?'

'I have no need of another branch of candles: these are quite sufficient.'

'Not if you are finding it a strain on your eyes.'

'I am not finding it a strain on my eyes.'

'Then why do you keep laying down your book and walking across to the windows?'

'You know as well as I!' There was a hint of irritation in Jack's voice. For what must have been at least the fifth time in the past hour, he twitched the curtains to one side and peered out into the darkening evening. 'He should have been back long since.'

'He is probably on his way at this very moment.'

'Yes! That is what you said half an hour ago.—It will be dark as pitch before we know it.'

'One has to remember—' Fanny paused, delicately—

'that he is doubtless more *accustomed* than you to be riding about in the darkness.'

'Not on a night when there is no moon! He may be a maniac, but he is not a complete idiot.'

'Well, then, in that case the mare has most likely gone lame, or cast a shoe, or—'

'She has not cast a shoe! He had her shod only yesterday. As for going lame—' Jack let fall the curtain, impatiently—'he will be lucky if she doesn't break her neck, and his along with it, and serve him right if she does! I wish to God he had taken the carriage as I wanted him to do.'

'Why would he not?'

'Oh, some cock and bull tale about not liking to be shut in. It was only an excuse. I saw through it on the instant. He cannot bear to think that an opportunity might come his way and he not be in a position to grasp it. I tell you, it has become as bad as that! He does it purely and simply for the sake of it.'

'Does what?' said Fanny, wrinkling her brow. 'What are you talking about?'

'What do you suppose that I am talking about? People in carriages,' said Jack, 'cannot hold up other people who are in carriages . . . one must needs be on horseback for such kind of activity.'

'Now you are being unfair!'

'Am I?'

'Yes, you are! You know that you are! He gave you his assurance, there would be no more of it.'

'*That* was conditional upon Miss Fredericks' accepting him.'

'Which she will have done—you may take my word on it.'

'Then where the devil is he?'

'Have you considered the possibility,' said Fanny, 'that they may have prevailed upon him to stay overnight?'

'Yes—and dismissed it! Had that happened, he would have let us know. He would have arranged for a messenger to be sent over. In any case—'

'In any case nothing.' Fanny spoke firmly. 'You are lashing yourself to no purpose. He is a grown man of eight and twenty and is perfectly capable of looking after himself. There is no need at all for all this breast beating.'

'That is not the impression you gave the other night, when you were working yourself up into a state!'

'The other night,' said Fanny, 'we had not the least idea where he was nor what he was doing. Tonight we know that he has gone to visit the woman he loves and to make her a proposition of marriage. In the circumstances, it is scarcely to be wondered at if he is a trifle late.'

'A *trifle* late? He is—'

'—far more than a trifle! I am very conscious of it. You have my most sincere apologies.'

'Richard!' Jack spun around, relief and accusation both evident in his voice. 'Where the devil have you been?'

'I was unavoidably detained. I came as fast as I could, and now, with regrets, must go again, and as speedily as possible. Fanny—' he held out his hands—'forgive me! I would not have risked coming here at all, were it not for the fact that I knew you would be worried.'

'Worried!' Jack gave a short laugh. 'It is not Fanny who has been worried. *She* has been the one to be finding excuses for you . . . the mare has gone lame, or has cast a shoe, or—'

'No, no, sweetheart! The mare is not to blame—and you need not take fright that anyone will see her. I have tethered her to some bushes further down the lane. She is well enough hidden. It will be better, however, if I get away immediately. I will just go and snatch up my bags and then I will be off.'

'You will do no such thing!' Jack's voice rang out, harshly. He was across the room in three quick strides, slamming the door shut even as Richard had it open. 'There are limits to one's patience! I do not care how long we have known each other nor what degree of friendship we have enjoyed, I will not stand by and have my wife insulted and my hospitality abused. So long as you are under my roof, you will be good enough to conduct yourself in a civilised fashion!'

Richard's lips twisted in a slight, derisive mockery of a smile.

'Alas, it would seem that I am not capable . . . which is

the very reason I would absent myself, and with all possible speed to spare you embarrassment.'

He turned, and would have wrenched open the door, but that Jack still had a hand on it.

'You had better let me go,' he said.

'I will do no such thing! Not until I have received a civil explanation from you!'

'Come, man! Don't be a fool! Stand away from that door.'

'Oh? So you would threaten me now? And in my own house?'

'I am not threatening you; merely asking you to let me go.'

'And I am telling you that I have not the least intention of so doing!'

'You would keep me against my will? What kind of friendship is that?'

'Friendship which has reached the end of its tether! I have put up with a great deal over the years, but by God, this time I mean to extract a little common courtesy!'

'If I were you, I should forget about common courtesy and think of your wife and children. You will do well to let me go.'

'I will not.'

'Damn you, Jack! Stand aside!'

It was as well the injunction was ignored. As Richard lunged forward, he seemed first to sway, and them to stagger: the blow that was intended for Jack never reached him.

'You damned—stiffnecked—fool—' Richard crumpled, slowly, into his friend's waiting arms. 'Whatever you do, don't keep me here . . . for the love of God . . . don't keep me!'

All very well; what else were they to do? Even if Jack might have hardened his heart, Fanny would not hear of it.

'Where is he to go if he does not stay with us? Who else is there to take care of him? We are the only family that he has.'

'He should have thought of that before he got himself into this predicament—whatever precisely it may be. I would remind you that we do not yet know what it is he has done.'

'I don't care what he has done! He is in no state to be riding anywhere.'

'Obviously not, just at this present moment. I will give him another twenty-four hours, and then—'

'Twenty-four hours? When he has had a *bullet* put through him?'

'The wound is clean. It will heal very quickly. Besides, he has the constitution of an ox.'

'Yes,' said Fanny, 'and the sensitivity of a human being . . . something has obviously gone very wrong between him and Miss Fredericks. Even if he is *physically* fit to go off, he will not be *emotionally* so. Only think how you would have it on your conscience if you were to turn him away and in his desperation he did something utterly foolish and got himself killed!'

Jack was none too sure that he would have it on his conscience, but it never did to argue with Fanny in one of her more fiercely maternal moods. He shrugged his shoulders, therefore, and said that for his part he washed his hands of the whole business.

'If anyone comes looking for him, I shall deny all knowledge.'

'Well, of course you will!' said Fanny. She sounded indignant. 'You don't imagine that I would let you meekly hand him over? *That* would be as wicked as sending him away.'

To begin with, at any rate, there could be no question of sending him away. For all that the bullet had passed clean through, the wound became infected: for the first twenty-four hours he lay muttering, in a fever, talking deliriously of things that made no sense. They watched over him anxiously, scared to call in a doctor lest it put him in jeopardy—scared *not* to do so for the self-same reason. Fortunately, five years of spartan living had had the effect of toughening, rather than weakening, what was a naturally strong constitution; by the end of the second day the patient was sufficiently recovered to be rational once more. Jack stood at the foot of the bed, looking down at him.

'How do you feel?'

'As weak as a kitten, dammit! I can't even sit up. Why the devil you would not let me go when I asked—'

'If I had, you would only have collapsed on the doorstep.'

'Then you might have kicked me outside and left me to get on with it. It is what I would have done in your place.'

'Yes, but you see, you are not in my place . . . you do not have a friend who is for ever causing you distress by reason of his reckless and immoderate behaviour, nor a harridan of a wife who refuses to hear a word against him.'

'No, by God! You're right.' Richard abandoned his attempts at sitting up and fell back again against the pillows. 'I have neither the one nor the other, nor now am ever like to have.'

There was a silence.

'What, exactly, went wrong?' Jack drew up a chair to the side of the bed. "Do you feel able to tell me?'

'Oh! I conducted myself like a benighted idiot, that is all . . . threw caution to the winds and paid the price. I came within ame's ace of being recognised.'

Jack raised an eyebrow.

'How so?'

'My own carelessness entirely.—I was in two minds whether to come back to Twelvetrees at all. That is why I skulked around until dark and left the mare—the mare!' In his agitation, Richard achieved what had previously defeated him, and shot up out of the bed. 'Jack! The mare!'

'Calm yourself . . . I had her brought back to the stables that same night.'

'But if someone had come looking—'

'I should have said that we found her running loose. We do not all of us lose our heads in an emergency.—Lie down again before you open up that wound. That is better. Now, tell me who it is that may have recognised you.'

A scowl fixed itself upon Richard's face.

'Some canting fool by the name of Eve.'

'Tristram Eve?'

'Yes. Do you know him?'

'Not to speak to. He was there in Cheltenham that time,

as I recall, making himself popular with the ladies.'

'Was he so? I am glad to say I have no memory of it. He was certainly there this time, however.'

'This time? You never mean to tell me that you rode all the way to Ch—'

'No, no! When I say, *this t*—oh, never mind! It is of no importance. Suffice it to say that when the . . . incident occurred, I was not . . . correctly dressed for the part. It was just my cursed ill luck that *he* had to be the one to turn up—ay! And I would give a great deal to know what took him there, as well!'

Jack studied his fingernails.

'I suppose if I were to say "took him where?" you would only snap my head off and tell me that it was of no importance?'

The scowl intensified. There was a pause; then, in muttered tones: 'Boswood.'

'Boswood?'

'Ay! Boswood! That is what I said!'

'Very well. There is no need to shout.'

'I am not shouting! I am talking quite normally.'

'Then perhaps you would care to sink your voice to a whisper . . . walls do have ears, just as doors have keyholes . . . you have still not answered my original question, you know. When I asked you what went wrong, I was not referring to your . . . schoolboy pranks, so much as to your—shall we say, rather more *mature* activities?'

'If you are talking of Anne, you may as well save your breath: I have ruined myself with her. She has washed her hands of me, just as you would like to do if Fanny would only let you.—No!' (as Jack opened his mouth) 'You do not have to protest.'

'I was not going to do so.'

'Oh! Well! That is it, then. You were not going to do so. It proves my point.'

'On the contrary! It proves nothing at all—other than the fact that you have a penchant for jumping to the wrong conclusion. Are you sure you have not done so with Miss Fredericks?'

'When a man has the door virtually slammed in his face,

what other conclusion is he to jump to? Save the obvious one that he is not welcome?'

'What seems obvious is not necessarily what is correct.'

'No?' Then suggest me an alternative!'

'There could be all manner of alternatives . . . I believe I had better send Fanny in to see you. *She* will be able to think of some. If anyone can set you right, it will be Fanny.'

It was not often that Adam formally requested the pleasure of his sister's company. Anne was surprised, therefore, when Isabella one morning came to her with the news that 'Adam would like to see you in the library, if you think you should be able to spare him the time.'

She was very sure she would be able to spare him the time—since she had nothing more strenuous to do than arrange flowers in vases and play with the children, it would be a strange thing if she should not. She was at a loss, however, to think what he could possibly be wanting with her. Isabella pressed her hand, confidingly.

'I believe he has something of importance that he wishes to say to you . . . he has not told me what it is, but I am prepared to hazard a guess.'

'Then you are one step ahead of me,' said Anne, 'for I have not the faintest idea.'

She found Adam pacing the library. He seemed nervous, but that was nothing new. The least little thing, these days, was capable of causing anxiety. Quietly, as she did everything, Anne closed the door behind her.

'Isabella said that you wish to see me?'

'Yes!—Yes, that is correct. There is something I have to—that is, something I am charged with—that is—but why do you not come and sit down? Have this chair, it is better placed . . . there! That is it. Now you will be comfortable. You will not be in any draughts just there.—Will you take something to drink? A glass of ratafia, perhaps?'

She essayed humour: 'Not unless you think that I am like to have need of it!'

'Need of it?'

'To sustain me in my moment of shock . . . I begin to

think that what you have to say must be something very grave and terrible!'

'Not in the least. I cannot imagine what gave you *that* impression. It is serious, certainly—but will not, I trust, be in any way unwelcome. Indeed, from what Isabella tells me I am encouraged to believe that it will be just the opposite.'

Her heart *would* give a little leap, in spite of all resolutions to the contrary.

'In that case,' she said, lightly, 'I beg you will keep me in suspense no longer!'

'I had intended telling you yesterday, but then I did not. After the excitement of Sir Tristram's visit—well! The fact is, Sir Tristram has spoken to me. He wishes to know—wishes me to *ascertain*—whether you should have any objection—whether you should find it *agreeable*—in short,' said Adam, pulling a handkerchief from his sleeve, 'he is desirous of making you his wife.'

There was a long silence. Adam finished mopping his brow and put the handkerchief back in his sleeve.

'Well! And what do you think about that?' He sounded more confident now that he had said what had to be said. The glance he threw at Anne was triumphant rather than anxious. 'Sir Tristram to be wishing to make you his wife . . . such sort of an offer does not come every day of the week!'

Anne remained silent.

'Well?' Adam nodded, encouragingly. 'Have you no comment to make? No reflections to put forth?'

'The only reflection—' she spoke soberly—'which immediately occurs to me is that Sir Tristram might have done me the courtesy of coming to me direct.'

Adam flushed.

'It was no discourtesy that he did not.'

'Was it not?'

'No, indeed! It was intended rather as a mark of his consideration.'

'I see. I am a grown woman of four and twenty yet must be approached through my brother as if I were still a young girl of sixteen, with neither a mind nor a will of my own.'

'He did not mean to spring it on you, that is all! He wished you to have the opportunity of considering. Knowing your disposition as he does—'

'My disposition?' said Anne. 'What is my disposition?'

'He knows that you are nervous—easily upset—'

'How does he know that I am nervous and easily upset?' She rose from her chair, with unwonted vigour. 'Who has told him that I am? It certainly cannot be by his own observations, for when has *he* ever seen me scream or fall into a fainting fit? When has anybody ever seen me do so? When did *you* last know me to indulge in a bout of weeping or have recourse to the smelling salts? Do not accuse me of what I am not! I have faults enough without being saddled with weaknesses I do not possess.'

'I would not call them weaknesses—in a female they might almost be termed virtues, so long as they are kept within bounds. It is precisely this which concerns me! You say that you are not upset, but yet you quite plainly are. You have been so ever since your return from Cheltenham. The truth is, that you attempt too much—you push yourself too far! You must learn to recognise your own physical limitations. The fact that your constitution is not robust is nothing in the least to be ashamed of—indeed, to a man there is something very appealing in a woman's frailty. I daresay it is this very quality in you which has attracted Sir Tristram. He wishes to protect you, to—'

'I have no need of protection! I am not a piece of Dresden china and neither am I fashioned out of porcelain! I am made of solid flesh and blood, just as everyone else, and I grow impatient with being treated as if I were an invalid!'

'Well, well!' Adam's tone was conciliatory. 'We will forget that for now. I daresay Sir Tristram will know how to keep you in bounds . . . a woman will attend to her husband far more than to a mere brother!'

'Very possibly,' said Anne, 'but since I have not the least intention of marrying Sir Tristram, the situation will hardly arise.'

A frown appeared on Adam's face.

'This is not very moderate language . . . *not the least intention*? Here is no way to treat an offer of marriage!'

'I have not yet been made an offer; but seeing as Sir Tristram chooses to conduct his business through you, perhaps you will be kind enough to inform him that he will save us both a great deal of embarrassment by not pursuing the matter. I would not wish to be hurtful: you will know how to say it.'

The frown deepened.

'You mean to turn him down?'

'I am hopeful the necessity will not arise.'

'Come! This is not sensible! What possible grounds can you have?'

'None, save that I do not care for him and I do not wish to be married to him.'

'Tut! This is childish talk! You disappoint me—it is not at all what I expect.'

'In that case, I am sorry.'

'You are like to be! You are no longer a young girl, you know. You cannot afford to pick and choose as an eighteen-year old might do. Such an offer as Sir Tristram's is not like to come your way again.'

'I am aware of it.'

'Then will you not re-consider?—I am thinking of *you*.'

'If you are truly doing so, then I beg you will not press me.'

There was a pause; then Adam brought the flat of his hand down hard upon the mantelshelf.

'This is selfishness! It shows a lack of consideration which I would not have thought you capable of! You do not consider *me*—you do not consider Isabella! Can you suppose that it pleases me to see my own sister growing older year by year and still without those necessary adjuncts so indispensable to a woman's comfort and fulfilment? A husband to cherish her—children to solace—did not Isabella most selflessly dedicate her energies during the *entire duration* of your stay in Cheltenham to just this one end? And now you will throw it back in her face? You will negate all her efforts? Demonstrate your ingratitude by wilfully declaring you have *not the least intention* before you have even taken the trouble of thinking about it? This is what comes of surrounding someone with love and devotion . . . sooner or later, they grow indifferent—start to take it for granted—go their own way regardless and give not a jot for the feelings of others!'

Anne felt all the injustice of the words. In a low voice, she said: 'I did not mean to be ungrateful, and so little do I take for granted the kindnesses that you and Isabella show me that I have often been troubled in my mind whether I should remain here to be a burden on you. Indeed, I have recently given quite serious thought to going abroad to live with Aunt Sophie—you know that she has asked me many times. To *her,* at least, I could be useful. I should not need to feel myself for ever at the receiving end, nor causing distress by my selfishness.'

'There can, of course, be no question of selfishness.' Adam had sunk down at his desk, his head in his hands. 'That was ill said of me—I should not have used such a word. There is no one, I suppose, who could be called *less* selfish than you. As for going to live abroad—' wearily, he raised his head—'that is out of the question. Isabella would not hear of it. How would she manage if *you* were not here to bear her company and keep the children amused? With only such an old crotchet as I, her life would be dull indeed. Let us forget all that has been said. I will convey your feelings to Sir Tristram, and we must hope—' his head fell back again, into his hands—'we must hope that he takes it as a gentleman should.'

CHAPTER EIGHT

'You may preach caution,' said Fanny, 'just as much as you like: I cannot and *will* not continue to stand by and do nothing.'

'Your concern is laudable, but what exactly do you propose?'

'I shall call upon her. I shall ask if I may speak with her in private, and then I will ask her why it is that she sees fit to treat him in this fashion.'

'You will be treading on dangerous ground. Suppose the answer is that she has recognised him as the one who held up her carriage? It is what he himself fears.'

'Yes, because he can think of no other explanation.'

'And can you?'

'Not just at the moment. That is why I am going to speak to her. If she is half the woman he has led us to believe, she would hardly let a little thing like *that* put her off.'

'Oh! So you would call it a little thing now, would you? To ride about the country holding people up—'

'Richard does not ride about the country: he confines himself to one small area of it. Not that I am saying that makes it any *better*—'

'Not in the slightest!'

'—but anyone might know there has to be some good reason behind it. If Miss Fredericks truly loves him, she cannot suppose that he would indulge in such an activity from any base, or dishonourable, motive.'

'If she truly loves him, the shock has probably proved too much for her.'

'I don't think so,' said Fanny. 'She doesn't sound at all that sort of a young woman. From what Richard has told us, she is eminently sensible and level-headed.'

'I find *that* hard to believe, for a start! Eminently sensible and level-headed and lets herself get entangled with *him*? That is a likely tale!'

'Well, that is where you are wrong,' said Fanny, 'for *I* am sensible and level-headed and *I* have let myself get entangled—at any rate, to the extent where I care what becomes of him. That is why I refuse to sit back and do nothing whilst he slowly deteriorates. First thing in the morning, if you please, I shall take the carriage and go calling. I do not say that I will necessarily be able to make the situation any better, but one thing is certain: I cannot make it any *worse*.'

Three days had elapsed since the unwelcome revelation of Sir Tristram's matrimonial desires. For Anne, they had been three days of torment. Adam made no further reference to the subject and appeared to have dismissed it from his mind; she could tell, however, that he had not. She would catch him, at odd moments when he thought himself unobserved, frowning in her direction and drumming with his fingers, as if striving to work out the solution to some intractable problem. His anxiety on her behalf could not but strike her as excessive, but then so it always did. It was scarcely anything new. For all that, it could give her no pleasure, knowing him to be upset and herself to be the cause. She might have discussed the matter with Isabella, but that Isabella, for once, seemed disinclined, turning all

Anne's (admittedly tentative) overtures aside with either a nervous laugh or some totally irrelevant observation as to the state of the weather or the children's health. Anne was too shy to persist; and so it was talked about by none. Sir Tristram was not mentioned: neither was Richard.

They had now been back at Boswood for over a fortnight. Hope could not but diminish as the days increased, but yet she refused to relinquish it entirely. The secret must lie in keeping occupied—in not allowing herself to brood and grow morbid. To this end, she took to going off each morning for long walks across the park, accompanied only by Adam's two springer spaniels and occasionally, when he could be got off his cushions, by Isabella's pug. Isabella grumbled that she would "wear herself to a shadow . . . you are already quite thin enough as it is", whilst Adam worried lest she overtax her strength. She took no heed of either of them. If walking was necessary for her peace of mind, then walking was what she would do.

She was thus engaged one morning, stepping out across the grass, with the spaniels loping ahead and Pug panting at her side, when she heard the clatter of horse's hooves and the rumbling of carriage wheels along the drive. Her immediate thought (with sinking heart) was that it must be Sir Tristram come back to plague her. Either Adam had not yet written him, or if he had, the letter had evidently not been of sufficient forcefulness to deter. Frowning, she hurried on; but had scarcely gone more than a few yards before she found herself hailed:

'Miss Fredericks! It is Miss Fredericks, is it not?'

Anne stopped. A woman's voice? What women did she know? Other than Miss Morcomb, and it certainly was not *her*. Slowly, she turned. The carriage had come to a halt and its occupant was preparing to alight. A lady of about Anne's own age, neatly if not altogether stylishly attired in a demure poke bonnet and a round gown of pink cambric, stepped down on to the path. She was not a beauty, by any manner of means. Indeed, it had to be said that she was rather a plain lady, with a mouth somewhat on the largish side and teeth which could only be described as prominent. For all that, there was a something agreeable about her: her features might be homely, but they were far from displeasing. Anne recognised her at once as the lady who had been in Cheltenham on that first occasion, with Richard and his sister and the long, lanky gentleman with sandy-coloured hair. Richard had told her subsequently that the long, lanky gentleman was now become her husband; that they lived in a house called Twelvetrees, in the county of Gloucester, and had a nursery full of fine strapping infants.

'I hope one day that you may make their acquaintance, for Jack is the best and truest friend that any man could have, while as for Fanny, *she* is a treasure beyond all price.'

She was moving forward now, across the grass, seemingly impervious to the antics of the two spaniels, intent on rounding her up.

'Miss Fredericks! Forgive my accosting you in this barbaric fashion! It is quite unforgivable of me, especially when you do not even know who I am. Let me hasten to introduce myself.' She held out a gloved hand. 'I am Fanny Meldrum. I am not sure whether Richard—Mr Wykeham—may ever have mentioned me to you—'

'Many times!' Warmly, Anne took the hand that was being offered. 'Many, many times! Indeed, I have heard so much about you that I almost feel as if we were already acquainted.'

'Then we are in the same position, for I do not mind telling you that these past two weeks I have lived with Miss Anne Fredericks for breakfast, tea and dinner! It is, *Anne says this*, and *Anne does that*, until I have come to feel that I know you as well as if you were an old friend. It is that which prompted me to take the liberty of calling on you unannounced and then springing out when I saw you in the park . . . I knew at once it must be you! You are exactly as Richard has described you—which I confess somewhat surprises me, for in general he cannot tell even two minutes after meeting someone whether their hair is fair or whether it is dark, whilst as for remarking the colour of a person's *eyes*, that is a task completely beyond his normal capabilities!'

Anne blushed—was confused—knew not which way to look; and finally sought refuge in bending to pick up Pug, who had been scrabbling at her leg in a jealous bid for attention.

'Now that we have all the tiresome preliminaries over and done with,' said Fanny, 'we may talk and be companionable. Would it inconvenience you if we were to walk a little way? Just the two of us together?'

'No! Not at all. I should be only too happy.'

They set off across the park, the spaniels bounding ahead once more, with Pug, back on the ground, grunting and snuffling at Anne's side.

'I had hoped that I should be able to speak with you alone. Indeed, I came here expressly for that purpose. I think you will probably have guessed—' Fanny paused, gravely—'what it is I wish to ask you. You will perhaps wonder by what right I do so, particularly when Richard has not the least notion that I am here and would doubtless be excessively angry if he were to discover, for if there is one thing he will not tolerate it is people meddling in his affairs, but the fact is that if *I* do not speak up for him he will never do it for himself . . . Miss Fredericks—Anne! I may call you Anne, may I not? And you will call me Fanny, since we feel ourselves both so well acquainted with each other already—Anne, I cannot tell you how it has been with him these past few days . . . he set out last Thursday as one who walks on air—and came back to us utterly shattered! He has been so ever since. He is convinced that he has ruined himself with you—that you will have no more to do with him. Is it so, Miss Fredericks?—Anne! Has he indeed ruined himself? Irrevocably and for all time? Was it truly by your orders that the door was shut? I cannot believe—speaking to you now—being with you—seeing you—I cannot believe that it was! I cannot believe that you would be so cruel as to do such a thing! Whatever he may have said, or done, to give offence, I assure you—' She broke off. 'I have said too much! I see by your expression—I have offended you myself. Miss Fredericks—'

'Anne!'

'Anne . . . I do most earnestly entreat you to forgive me if I have gone too far! It is only—'

'You have not gone too far—indeed, you have not gone nearly far enough, for what you say makes no sense! When you speak of last Thursday—of doors being shut—and by *my* orders—I gave no such orders!'

'I knew you had not! Oh! I knew it could not be you!'

'I think,' said Anne, sombrely, 'that there is some mystery here which needs unravelling. Last Thursday I was in Oxford, with my sister-in-law.'

'Yes! That is what he was told . . . that you were in Oxford and were not expected back until later in the afternoon. That in itself could not but strike him as odd, for after all he had been invited, but then when your brother refused even to see him—'

'Refused to see him?' Anne echoed the words, in astonishment. 'Adam? And you say that he had been *invited?*'

'It was to have been a surprise, for your birthday—a plot hatched between him and your sister-in-law. Naturally, at first, he assumed she had simply forgot—'

'Which would have been quite bad enough in itself!'

'Well, it would,' agreed Fanny, 'but such things happen, and at least it would not be the same as if *you* had forgot. It was only when your brother would not see him and suggested he may perhaps have made a mistake in the name that he realised he was being deliberately—well! Discouraged, shall we say? You may imagine how it made him feel!'

'Yes.' Anne bent her head. A tremor ran through her. Last Thursday had been the day Sir Tristram had arrived—unexpectedly, or so Adam had claimed. Was it possible (the thought came to her only with the greatest of reluctance) was it possible Adam had known in advance of Sir Tristram's intended visit? That for some reason he had wished the field to be kept clear? Alas! In the light of what had occurred subsequently, it began to appear all too probable. Adam was strong for Sir Tristram: he would naturally support *his* claims above those of a young man entirely unknown to him. But for Isabella—for *Isabella* to be party to it!

Anne covered her face with her hands. Such sort of treachery could not easily be forgiven. Adam's high-handedness might rankle: Isabella's betrayal could only hurt.

'My dear!' Fanny's tone was compassionate. 'I had not

intended to upset you. I wished only to ascertain, for Richard's sake, whether he might still hope, or whether all was irretrievably lost. I would not for the world have caused you any distress!'

It was a moment before Anne could bring herself to reply; then: 'I assure you—' she spoke earnestly—'whatever distress I may feel *now* is as nothing to the distress that I was feeling before. When one has managed to convince oneself that one has been . . . forgotten—'

'Forgotten? Never! He speaks of you incessantly! If you only knew how miserable he has been since last Thursday!'

Anne's lips curved, rather tremulously, into a smile.

'Perhaps you may like to tell him, how miserable *I* have been.'

'I will! Be very sure I will! *Now* I shall not mind his knowing that I have dared to come here. When he hears the news I bring him, I rather fancy he will find it in himself to forgive me . . . not, of course,' said Fanny, cheerfully, 'that it will make him *happy* to know you have been suffering, but at least, perhaps, it will help take the scowl from his face and the wrinkles from his brow! There is only one thing that troubles me, and that is whether I am to advise him to try calling upon you again, or whether there is some reason for your brother not wishing him to be encouraged?'

'There is only one reason that I can think of,' said Anne, soberly, 'and that is that my brother is strongly in favour of my accepting a proposal of marriage from a gentleman who is an acquaintance of his. I have made it very plain—*very* plain!—that I cannot do so, but I believe secretly he still cherishes the belief that I may have a change of heart. I can think of nothing else which could even begin to explain such extraordinary behaviour on his part, for truly it *is* extraordinary. Anyone might be entitled to conclude that he is just a boor, but I promise you he is not!'

'I am very sure he is not. What you have said sounds all too probable . . . I remember *my* brother once took violent exception to the fact that one of my sisters refused to marry the man of his choice—*his* choice, you will note!—and threatened quite seriously to take a riding crop to any other creature of the male sex who dared show himself within a ten-mile radius! Brothers are inordinately possessive where sisters are concerned. I sometimes think they are worse than fathers, for fathers, being older, tend in general to adopt a somewhat more philosophical attitude. It will obviously be more diplomatic for the moment if Richard does *not* come hammering at your door. The last thing he must be wishing to do is make an enemy of your brother—and yet I know very well he will not rest content until he has been able to see you and talk with you! Miss Fredericks—Anne!—what are we to do? Can we hatch up a scheme between us, do you think?—or should you not like to do what your brother might disapprove of?'

'As a rule, I should not,' said Anne, 'but in this instance it seems he leaves me no choice . . . I am perfectly agreeable to hatch up any scheme that you wish.'

'Very well.' Fanny slipped a companionable hand through her arm. 'Let us put our heads together and see what brilliant contrivance we may come up with . . .'

'I think you will agree,' said Anne (looking severely across the room at a red-eyed Isabella) 'that it is the least you can do . . . you were quick enough, after all, to arrange a trip into Oxford when it suited *your* purposes.'

'They were not my p-purposes.' Isabella dabbed piteously at her eyes with a small square of linen. 'They were your b-brother's. *He* was the one who said I must d-do it.'

'I am aware of that, but it is no excuse. He could not *force* you into it.'

'No, but he could t-talk me into it. He managed to convince me that it was for your own g-good. I should not have done it otherwise . . . Anne, you *c-cannot* marry Mr Wykeham!'

Anne tilted her chin.

'Mr Wykeham has not yet asked me to do so.'

'N-no, but if he d-does—'

'Yes?' Her tone was militant. 'If he does?'

'You must r-regretfully d-decline.' Isabella blew her nose on the scrap of linen. 'It is for your own g-good.'

'I am rather tired,' said Anne, 'of being told that this or

that is for my own good. I am four and twenty years of age and am perfectly capable of deciding such things for myself.'

'Not—' Isabella hiccuped—'not unless you are in f-full possession of the f-facts.'

'Which facts do you speak of?'

'The facts about Mr W-Wykeham . . . Anne, he has had to be c-conf-*fined* all these years!'

There was a slight pause; then: 'How do you mean, confined?'

'C-conf-fined—sh-shut up—'

'Shut up where?'

'I d-don't know . . . wherever they d-do shut people up when they lose their powers of r-reason.'

Anne's cheek grew pale.

'Where did you hear this?'

'It was Adam—*he* knew of it.' Again, Isabella dabbed at her eyes. 'You know Adam is not one for r-romancing. If *he* s-says a thing is s-so—'

If Adam said a thing was so, then it could be taken as a virtual certainty that it was so.

Anne bit her lip.

'I am sure it is t-terribly s-sad,' said Isabella, 'but now that you have been enl-lightened—'

'Now that I have been enlightened, can you suppose it makes an atom of difference? When tragedies occur, some people are harder hit than others—you have only to look at Adam to see that. That is no reason for dismissing them.'

'I am n-not dismissing him! I am only saying that you cannot m-*marry* him.'

'And I am saying that I shall most certainly do so if he asks me—just as *you* are most certainly coming into Oxford with me the day after to-morrow.'

'But we cannot have another sh-shopping trip s-so soon!'

'Oh, but we can,' said Anne. 'I have it all arranged . . . we are going into Oxford in order that you may change your nice new bonnet for an even nicer one which you saw the other day but were too scared to buy, on account of its being so expensive . . . that shall be your reward for helping me, and the price that Adam must pay for trying to run my life.

He is getting off rather lightly, but I have no wish to be malicious . . . I would only counsel you to buy the most expensive bonnet that you can find, for I daresay it may be some little while before he lets you go again!'

CHAPTER NINE

'I remember,' said Richard, 'the very first occasion on which I saw you . . . you were wearing a dress made of some lilac material and had a bonnet to match, trimmed with pink rosebuds.'

Anne suppressed a shudder.

'I would far rather you had forgot it!'

'I have forgotten nothing about that first occasion. I remember you were carrying a parasol—'

'Do not tell me! The parasol was also lilac?'

'Yes, it was. The whole ensemble was lilac. It is a colour I have always associated with you.—Do you remember where it was we first met? It was in the Pump Room—'

'I remember *that.*'

'I was on my way in, as you were on your way out . . . you had been elbowed to one side by a parcel of roughs and were in danger of falling.'

'And you put out your arm to save me—'

'As it seems that I must do yet again!' Just in time, Richard caught her about the waist and swung her out of the path of an oncoming vehicle, driven at spanking pace down the main street by a young buck wearing a striped coat with buttons the size of soup plates. 'Damned idiot!' Richard shook his fist, then turned, anxiously, to look down at Anne. 'Are you all right? You are not hurt?'

'No thanks to myself.' Anne laughed, rather shakily. 'I am not as a rule so stupid. I cannot think what came over me.'

'It was not your fault. People have no right to go at such a speed through the centre of a town.'

'It might be said that people have no right to go stepping into roads without first taking a look to see if there is anything approaching . . . I think my head must be up in the clouds! I have never done such a thing in my life before.'

'Hm!' Richard grunted, and pressed a hand, for a moment, to his side. 'Just so long as you have . . . taken no hurt.'

'*I* have not.'

'No, no! And neither have I! You must not be worried by this: it is an old wound that has not yet healed.'

'Old?' said Anne. Her brow wrinkled.

'Old enough. I have lived a lifetime since sustaining it. Desperation, despair, self-pity . . . I have been through them all this past week, when I have thought myself rejected by you. Now that you have given me reason to hope once more, I will heal very speedily.—Why do you look at me like that? You have a quizzical air! Do you not believe that I have been in desperation and despair? If that is the case, then let me tell you that this injury of mine may be attributed *directly* to the hopeless state into which I was thrown after my dismissal from Boswood. If you could only picture to yourself the misery—the sheer and utter misery!—into which I was plunged—the despondency which engulfed me as I thought never to see you again—why, then, you would not wonder that I did something foolish.'

'Foolish! You surely do not mean—'

'That I tried to put a period to my existence? There are some who might see it in that light. It is not the way *I* saw it—or at any rate, not at the time. I only knew that I was half crazed by what had occurred and that it led me into committing an act of the greatest folly, which I assure you I am now heartily ashamed of. One of these days, perhaps, when I can speak more rationally, I will tell you about it. Just at this moment, it causes me too acute an embarrassment. Let us talk of you rather than of me.' He drew Anne's arm through his. 'I could scarcely believe it when I saw you were come back to Cheltenham! All those years of fruitless searching—and suddenly, there you were! I recognised you at once. You have changed not one jot. You are just as I have always remembered you—and pray do not tell me that my memory is false! You were fair and slender when I first met you, and you are fair and slender still. However jealously I might seek for signs of change, not one line or wrinkle can I discern . . . here you behold *me,* a perfect wreckage, and there are you, as fresh and blooming as the day I first set eyes on you.'

Anne smiled.

'I think I must allow for some slight exaggeration—unless, of course, your sight is not what it was!'

'I thank you! My sight is in no way deteriorated—and neither are *you.* I only wish that I might know the secret of it!'

'There is no secret. If I remain relatively unchanged it is because the sort of life I have been leading has not been conducive to change. I have done nothing to incur it—I have been nowhere, met no one. Had I led a more rough and tumble kind of existence, I daresay you would see the marks of it.'

'Even as *you* can see the marks on me. You would say, no doubt, that I had led a pretty rough and tumble kind of existence?'

Anne hesitated.

'Would you not? If you were to be honest?'

'If I were to be honest, I . . . am not quite sure what I would say.'

'I see! You will not commit yourself. You will not be brave enough to take a stand and to state firmly and unequivocally that this young man—except that now, alas, he is no longer quite so young!—this young man has plainly led a life of extreme debauchery and dissipation.'

'No,' said Anne. 'Are you saying that I ought?'

'Oh! I would not presume to dictate to you. Only—' Quite suddenly, he stopped. 'Does it bother you,' he said, 'not to know where I have been, and what I have been doing, during these years that we have been apart?'

'If it had bothered me,' said Anne, calmly, 'I should have asked you.'

'You mean that you would entrust yourself to me without knowing?'

'I mean that you do not have to explain anything unless you wish to do so.'

They walked on a while in silence.

'The fact is,' said Richard, abruptly, 'that I have been looking for a murderer.'

'Looking for a murderer?' It was Anne's turn to stop. 'Can you be serious? What kind of a murderer?'

'There is only one kind of a murderer: a person who murders someone.'

'But—'

'Five years ago,' said Richard, 'someone murdered my sister. I swore then that I would bring him to book if it were the last thing that I did . . . that is the somewhat ignoble task to which I have devoted myself: the pursuit of vengeance. Fanny would be angry if she knew that I had told you. She would say that I will have only myself to blame if you take me for a raving lunatic and refuse to have anything more to do with me. But I cannot help it! That is a risk that I shall have to run. I have no alternative. I cannot ask you to be my wife if all is not made clear.—Anne!' He caught her by the shoulders, pulling her towards him. 'Tell me that I have not ruined my chances . . . tell me that you, at least, do not consider me a madman!'

'If I did, I give you my word, I should by now be screaming at the top of my voice!'

'And suppose I were to ask you to become my wife? Would you do so?'

'Most willingly!'

'You would marry me and make a reformed character of me?'

'If that is what you want.'

'It is what I want! I grow weary of this constant ache for revenge. It is time I learnt to forget, if not to forgive!'

'You mean,' said Anne, '—or at least, I think you do—that it is time you learnt to forgive, if not to forget.'

'Forgive? No! That is something I can never do!'

'But surely—' Anne's voice was gentle, yet not without a hint of reproach—'surely whoever it was that caused the tragedy of your sister's death did so quite accidentally? There was no malicious intent?'

'There may have been no malicious intent: the result was still the same. Had he stood his ground, like a man, it would have been a different matter. To turn and run was the act of an arrant coward and as such deserves nothing but contempt.'

'It is certainly not easy to feel any great degree of pity—'

'Pity!'

'—but has it not occurred to you,' said Anne, 'that this person, whoever he was, may have suffered his own torments all these years? That just as *you* have been racked by the desire for revenge, so *he* may have been torn apart by guilt and remorse?'

'If that were the case, there has been nothing to stop him coming forward and declaring himself. I am sure he knows very well how he may find me. *He* does not have to go in search: he has but to show himself. I will know him.'

'Can you really be so sure?' said Anne. 'After so long an interval of time?'

Richard gave a short laugh.

'I can be sure . . . not of his face, for I caught but a fleeting glimpse of it. I would hesitate to condemn any man on that evidence alone. But a certain face in conjunction with a certain deformity . . . a man may hide his chin beneath a beard, or cover his baldness with a wig, but if he has only three fingers on one of his hands there is nothing very much that he can do to disguise it. And be it in ten years' time, or be it in twenty, I shall know him. Let there be no mistake about that: I shall know him—and I shall give him no quarter! On the surface I may learn to forget; but forgive—never! Never if I live to be as old as Methuselah! The fact that he chooses to remain in hiding only adds fuel to the flames. It only increases the contempt in which I—Anne! Good God! What is wrong? You have turned as white as a sheet! Are you feeling unwell?'

She had never felt more so. A *man may hide his chin beneath a beard, or cover his baldness with a wig*... Her head swam, the world turned somersaults before her. Valiantly she struggled, but in vain: were it not for the support of Richard's arm about her waist, she must have sunk to the ground where she was.

'Let me take you back straight away to your sister-in-law! You are quite obviously feeling poorly.'

She could not deny it. She trembled as she walked, and for all the determination of her efforts could make no pretence at being otherwise.

'My dearest Anne!' Isabella cried out in alarm as she saw her approach. A bonnet which she had been about to try on, an elaborate creation of swirling satin and tulle, dropped insensibly from her hands. Fanny caught at it just in time. 'Whatever is the matter? You are shaking all over! Have you taken a chill?'

'That is maybe—what it is—' She managed, somehow, to get the words out. 'The wind is—quite strong—'

'I ought never to have kept you out there for so long!' Richard's arm tightened remorsefully about her. 'It is my fault. You should have stopped me! You are not accustomed to be walking for miles at a stretch.'

'That is just the problem.' Isabella spoke accusingly. 'It is just what she *is* accustomed to. She has done nothing this past week but tramp about the grounds. It is not to be wondered at if she has knocked herself out. I told her she would do so. If only she would sometimes listen to me, but no, she must always know best! Now see what you have done! Overtaxed your strength and made yourself ill.'

'I wish you will take her back home,' said Richard, 'and make sure that she rests.'

'Oh! I shall make sure of it. This time she shall do as *I* say, and there shall be no argument about it. I will brook no opposition!'

Anne was in no state to be offering any: she longed only for the privacy of her own room. As he handed her into the waiting carriage, Richard pressed her hand with a murmured 'We will contrive another meeting, just so soon as you are well again. In the meantime, you must not worry yourself. Only concentrate upon regaining your strength: *that* is the sole thing that matters.'—She lowered her gaze, and knew not how to answer him.

The drive back to Boswood, with Isabella alternately solicitous and scolding, was a species of nightmare. Her spirits sank lower even as physically she grew stronger. By the time Boswood was reached she was feeling very nearly restored as far as her *bodily* self was concerned: it was mentally, now, that she suffered.

'You will go straight upstairs,' said Isabella. 'I will accept no excuses.'

Anne was not making any. Her room was a haven: she could not wait to be in there. When Adam met her on the front steps with the news that 'Sir Tristram is come again. I am sorry if you do not like it, but that is how it is,' she did not hesitate.

'I do not like it and have no intention of seeing him. I have the headache and am going to my room, You may tell him what you wish. It is up to you.'

'But, Anne, this is not good enough! He is come especially.'

'I cannot help that. I will not see him.'

'Anne!'

Adam laid his hand, reproachfully, upon her arm. A tremor ran through her: she could not help it. *A man may hide his chin beneath a beard, or cover his baldness with a wig; but if he has only three fingers on one of his hands*—

'I am sorry.' Stiffly, Adam withdrew. He had always been sensitive about his deformity; the only difference was, that never before had Anne shown herself affected by it.

'I am going to my room.' She turned, deliberately, to the stairs. 'If Sir Tristram is here in the morning, perhaps I shall see him then.'

'So!' Fanny, at her most severe, settled back into the corner of the carriage as it rolled towards Twelvetrees. 'Do you intend telling me what happened?'

'How do you mean?'

'Come! Don't fence! You know very well what I mean . . . what did you do to her, to make her so upset?'

'What did I do?' Richard sounded indignant. 'I did nothing at all! We were getting on famously. Fanny, she has said that she will be my wife! She is—'

'Yes, yes! Of course she has said that she will be your wife! The poor girl cannot help herself: she is head over heels in love with you.'

'And I with her! It is no one way thing.'

'Then in that case, why did you upset her?'

'I did not upset her! We were standing there talking, when quite suddenly she grew faint.'

'Miss Fredericks is not the sort of young woman who *quite suddenly grows faint*—not unless there is a very good reason. What were you talking about?'

'Oh—' Richard looked uncomfortable. 'This and that.'

'Be more specific, if you please!'

'I was merely telling her—'

'Telling? What?'

'About . . . where I have been—what I have been doing—'

'*What?*' Fanny jerked forward on her seat. 'You mean you have actually told her of your activities? That you have been riding about the country holding people—'

'No, no! Not that! At least—not in so many words. Do you take me for an idiot?'

Fanny looked at him, rather hard.

'You do—quite obviously! I am not, however. I merely told her that I had been—searching for someone.'

'And she did not wish to know who, or why, or anything about him?'

'Well—yes. She was naturally curious.'

'So you, naturally, gave her all the details?'

'There can be no harm in that!'

'You think not? You think it is what a young girl *likes* to hear from the man she is in love with and has pledged herself to marry? That he is still thirsting for revenge for an accident which occurred five years ago? That his one obsessive aim in life is the pursuit of some unknown man with half a finger missing? A finger which he *himself* has shot off? You think this is likely to rouse her sympathy? You think she will find it either laudable or romantic? I am not in the least surprised she turned faint! She must begin to wonder what kind of a monster she has got herself entangled with! Good God in heaven! Have you no sensitivity? You know perfectly well it is a subject on which you can never speak calmly! You have very likely frightened the poor girl half to death with your rantings and ravings!'

There was a silence. Richard looked crestfallen.

'I had not seen it in that light.'

'No . . . it is amazing how gentlemen seem to take it for granted that we women share in their bloodthirsty cravings.'

'I have no bloodthirsty cravings!'

'Oh? I had always understood that when you finally caught up with your quarry the intention was to run him through without mercy?'

Richard flushed.

'That was said in a moment of passion. I would obviously give the man a fair chance.'

'You mean you would challenge him to fight a duel? I hope you did not tell Miss Fredericks *that.*'

'Er—no. No, I did not say that.'

'So what did you say?'

He swallowed.

'I merely said that I—would give him no quarter.'

Fanny closed her eyes.

'It is not as bad as it seems! Fanny, believe me! I was not vicious—my language was not immoderate! I spoke quite calmly, quite collectedly—'

'Just as you are doing now, I suppose. So calmly and collectedly that you have obviously managed to convince her that you are ripe for the madhouse.'

Richard's face was drawn.

'You think that I have indeed upset her?'

'I think you have very little understanding of how to treat a lady. You have lived apart from us for too long. You cannot spend five years out of society and return to it as polished as when you went away. There are things you have forgotten, which you will need to set about re-learning.'

'Will she still give me the chance, do you think?'

'She will be a woman in a thousand if she does. But then—' Fanny relented—'since I am much inclined to believe that she *is* a woman in a thousand—'

'She is! I give you my word!'

'In that case,' said Fanny, 'you have answered your own question.'

CHAPTER TEN

'Where is Anne?' said Adam. 'Have you seen her this morning?'

'Anne? Why—no! That is—' Isabella hesitated. 'I hope you are not going to bully her?'

'I have not the least intention of bullying her! Sir Tristram is wishing to take her for a drive, that is all.'

'I am sure that is very kind of Sir Tristram, but this is her day for seeing Miss Morcomb. Anne is very fond of Miss Morcomb. I do not think that even for Sir Tristram she would be willing to postpone. He cannot expect to descend upon people without warning and have them disrupt their entire schedule just to suit *his* convenience.'

'There is no question of disruption! Sir Tristram has very generously offered to convey her to Abingdon in his own carriage.'

'Oh! Well—in that case, perhaps—'

'In that case, perhaps, you will be good enough to inform me where she may be found!'

'I am not absolutely positive, but you might try the library. She mentioned something about writing a letter.'

'Writing a letter?' Adam frowned. 'Who has Anne to write letters to?'

'Who indeed?' said Isabella. 'Considering she is kept so cramped and confined here at Boswood.'

He flushed.

'It is for her own good. You know that as well as I!'

'Do I?' said Isabella. 'I sometimes begin to wonder. When she cannot even write a simple letter without arousing suspicion—'

'Who said anything about suspicion? What are you implying? Are you trying to tell me that she is writing to someone she ought not to be writing to?'

'She is four and twenty,' said Isabella. 'I should have thought, at four and twenty, one might write to whomever one chose.'

Anne was, indeed, engaged in the business of letter writing. He found her seated at a small table in a corner of the library, her head bent over a sheet of paper. As he entered the room, she looked up; and guiltily, as it seemed to him, spread her arm across the page to shield it from his gaze. For the moment, he let it pass.

'How are you feeling?' He closed the door behind him and crossed towards her. 'Is your headache gone?'

'I am glad to say so.'

'Good! Then hurry and make yourself ready . . . Sir Tristram is waiting to take you to Abingdon.'

'Sir Tristram? To Abingdon?'

'Yes, he has very kindly offered his services as escort.'

Anne pursed her lips.

'I am quite happy to go as I usually go; by myself. There is no need at all for him to be accompanying me.'

'No need, perhaps, except that he has offered . . . he wishes to enjoy the pleasure of your company! He wishes to be of service. There are some young women,' said Adam, 'who would be flattered.'

'I have been flattered enough. I grow weary of it.'

'Come!' Adam's face showed his displeasure. 'That is

scarcely very modest kind of talk.'

'I am not feeling very modest. I am feeling ill-used and hard done by.'

'This is nonsense!' cried Adam. 'Lay down your pen and go and put your bonnet on! Sir Tristram is waiting.'

'Then I am afraid that he must wait a while longer: I have not yet finished my letter.'

'What is this letter? With whom are you corresponding?'

Firmly, she kept the page hidden from his view.

'I believe that must be my business.'

'You would withhold it from me?' Adam's tone was cold, and accusing. 'You would quite openly conduct an illicit correspondence?'

'It is not illicit; but if it were, by your own actions you have left me no choice.'

'And, by God, by yours you leave *me* none! If you will not show me of your accord—' He thrust out a hand. 'Will you, or will you not?'

Anne said nothing.

'Then you give me no alternative!' He snatched up the letter. 'I will ask you one more time . . . do you intend telling me who your correspondent is, or must I read for myself and find out?'

'You have taken the letter by force. I cannot stop you reading it, if that is what you want.'

'It is not what I want! The very idea revolts me! But if you will not tell me what I quite legitimately wish to know—'

'Legitimately?' said Anne.

Her eyes met his. There was a silence; then Adam swallowed. Slowly he laid the sheet of paper back upon the table.

'Finish your letter. I will tell Sir Tristram you will be with him so soon as you are ready.'

'So!' Sir Tristram closed the lid of his snuff box, with a snap. 'She still does not co-operate.'

'She asked me to make her apologies. She is busy writing this letter. She will be with you just as soon as—'

'Yes, yes! So you have already said. I do not regard it as

very flattering to be told that a lady whom one is offering to escort will be with one *just as soon as.* It does not strike at all an encouraging note. In fact, just the opposite. I would almost go so far as to say it is an insult.'

'I assure you, she did not intend it as such.'

'Did she not? You must have a very poor opinion of my intellect if you think I will believe that . . . to whom, as a matter of interest, is she writing?'

'I—have really no idea. I did not feel it to be my business to inquire.'

'You lie,' said Sir Tristram. 'Your face betrays you. I thought you were supposed to have put a stop to all that?'

Adam spoke wretchedly.

'I thought that I had.'

'Then obviously you were mistaken, since now she writes letters to him . . . you fool! How come you to allow it?'

'I wish you will tell me how I am to prevent it! This is not the Middle Ages! I cannot force her to do my bidding.'

'You would sooner sit back and see her form an alliance with Richard Wykeham?'

'No!' A shudder ran through Adam's slight frame. 'Not that! That can never be!'

'Then it is in your own best interests, as well as hers, to ensure that it never is.'

'I have done as much as I can.' He pressed a hand to his face. 'Do not ask me to do more.'

Sir Tristram tapped thoughtfully with one slender finger upon the lid of his snuff box.

'I think you will admit,' he said, 'that I have been very patient thus far. I have not . . . pressurised you in any way. If I have made certain suggestions—put forward certain proposals—that is as far as I have gone. It has been entirely up to you whether you carried them out or not.'

'I have done my best! I cannot do more!'

'And I cannot remain patient indefinitely! I am not accustomed to be kept waiting. When I express a desire for something, I expect to be given it. If I am not given it—why, then!' Sir Tristram's hand closed like a vice over the snuff box. 'I take it!'

Adam raised his head.

'I will not force her. I have done her harm enough as it is . . . I will not use coercion!'

'And neither should I wish you to. In spite of what you may think, I am not a monster. It would give me no pleasure to be shackled to a wife who found me . . . uncongenial. But I do not believe that Miss Fredericks would do so. Were it not for a certain disturbing influence in her life, she would speedily come round to accepting the idea. The solution, therefore—' he paused—'would seem to be obvious: we must take steps to remove that influence.'

'Remove it?' Adam sounded uneasy. 'How do you mean, remove it?'

'Do I not make myself clear? Perhaps my choice of words is at fault. Perhaps I should have said . . . eliminate.'

'No!' Adam shook his head in violent negation. The cry seemed wrenched out of him. 'Not that!'

'Not?' Sir Tristram spoke with gentle mocking. 'But surely it is the solution to all our problems? Yours, as well as mine . . . only think how much easier your life would become! You might get out again—take your charming wife into company—drive about the country like a free man . . . come, my friend! If you do not care for *my* solution, then give me one of your own.'

'I cannot.' Adam sank down into a chair, his head in his hands. 'There is none—there has never been. What was done, was done. There can be no undoing it.'

'No undoing it—but at least a re-adjustment! The time is ripe! I am willing to relinquish my—advantages, shall we say? Yes! My advantages! I am willing to relinquish my advantages in order to gain your sister. It is up to you, therefore, to strike whilst the iron is hot. Do what has to be done, before the chance evaporates!'

'I?' Adam's face was ashen. The lines about his eyes and mouth seemed etched more deeply overnight. 'You would make me responsible for it?'

Sir Tristram spread his hands.

'Who else?' He smiled. 'You could hardly expect *me* to do the deed . . . I am perfectly willing to set it up for you, but I really do not think you can ask me to go any further . . . I am making sacrifice enough as it is!'

'Sacrifice!' Adam's tone was bitter. 'You have been bleeding me dry for years . . . I think you have had your money's worth.'

'I am inclined to agree with you. My nature is not a grasping one. That is why I am willing, now, to—ah—forgo my source of income and—' Sir Tristram waved a hand—'take your sister in exchange. All I require is that you perform this one small task.'

'It is no small task!' Adam was trembling. 'It is an act which fills me with horror and repulsion and it is no use demanding it of me for purely and simply I am not capable of it!'

'Strange,' murmured Sir Tristram, 'how you have changed with the years . . .'

'I have not changed! I have never been capable of such violence! I could no more kill a man on purpose than—'

'Than allow him to kill you? For I give you my word . . . oppose me in this, and that is what it will come to. What can be set up one way, can just as easily be set up another. And I do not think,' said Sir Tristram, 'that you would be much of a match for our young friend. He has been out for blood these past five years.'

'Then let him have it! My life is not so sweet that I will fight him for it.'

'No! And neither will the lives of your wife and children be so sweet, when once the truth is out . . . you would do well to consider *their* suffering, my friend, before so recklessly making up your mind to dispose of yourself.'

Adam moistened his lips.

'There would be no need for them to know.'

'Oh, but I should *arrange* for them to know! I think you will agree, it would scarcely be very fair to leave them in the dark. As for Miss Fredericks, I assure you,' said Sir Tristram, 'that it would afford me double pleasure to enlighten *her*.—Do you doubt me? No! Of course you do not. You would not be so foolish. Very well, then! Let us lay our plans. Tell me, first of all, where our friend may be got hold of. I presume he is still in the district?'

'I have not the least idea of his whereabouts.'

'Well! No matter. It is an easy enough thing to discover.

Miss Fredericks will either put her letter out for posting, in which case you may look at the direction; or, which is more likely, she will hand it to a servant for personal delivery—in which case, you may question the servant. It is scarcely any great stumbling block. Either way, you may rest assured he will not be so far afield he cannot be reached within the hour.'

Adam spoke in a low voice.

'What are you proposing?'

'All will become clear—Miss Fredericks will help us! At what hour does she commonly arrive back from her visits to Abingdon?'

Adam swallowed.

'In general, between seven and—and eight o'clock.'

'Between seven and eight o'clock . . . suppose on this occasion we stipulate for eight? Eight strikes me as being a reasonable sort of hour. Not yet dark, but sufficiently dusky to encourage those whom one would wish to encourage . . . so! Assuming the journey to take—what shall we say? Thirty minutes? I know, since your accident, you do not care to drive fast—'

'I do not care to drive at all! In fact—' Adam was twisting his hands in agitation—'in fact, I will not do so! I have taken a vow! I will not break it! I will not—'

'Calm yourself! Calm yourself!' Sir Tristram spoke soothingly. 'There is no need for you to break it. If you do not care to drive, then let yourself be driven. Let your coachman take you.'

'But if he is there, what need have I to go? He is perfectly capable of fetching her back by himself. It is what he is accustomed to do!'

'And is he also accustomed,' wondered Sir Tristram, 'to meet up with masked men upon the highway?—You start! I see that you begin to perceive my drift . . . we offer you as bait—what could possibly be simpler? The lure, I fancy, will prove well nigh impossible for our bloodthirsty young friend to resist. He will come post haste, he will find you waiting—and the rest is up to you. You must indicate to me, by the by, where there is a spot that would be suitable. We do not want you taken by surprise. Tell me where you will like the incident to occur, and I will pinpoint it on my way into Abingdon this morning, then on my return journey I can time myself—I take it your coachman does not drive like a Jehu? No; I thought not. Very well, I will moderate my pace to something approaching the funereal. That way, we should be able to give our friend a fairly accurate indication of when you are likely to be passing. It would be a pity, after all our careful planning, if he were to arrive too late—and do not, I beg of you, ask me "too late for what?" as I see by your expression that you are about to do! I think you know very well what is required of you. Just have your pistols ready primed, and be on the alert. I realise you are no hero—' Adam flinched, visibly—'but this is a case where not even a ten-year old schoolboy could fail. So long as you keep your head, there is nothing that can go wrong.'

The journey to Abingdon was pursed very largely in silence. Anne was bound up in her own thoughts; Sir Tristram seemed determined on a new policy of not speaking until he was spoken to. Occasionally he would pass some comment on the scenery, or the state of the road, but they were not such as called for any great effort of reciprocity on Anne's part: she might get away very well with the odd 'Yes, indeed!' or 'Is it not?' Only once did he make any attempt to engage her in sustained conversation.

'That is the place they call Hangman's Hill, is it not?' He was leaning forward, nodding through the window at a distant clump of trees that topped a slight rise in the ground.

'I believe it is,' said Anne.

'Have you any idea why?'

'None, I am afraid.'

'One would imagine there must have been a gibbet there, at some time.'

'It is always possible.'

'Of course, you would not approve of gibbets, would you, Miss Fredericks?'

'I do not, as it happens.'

'I knew you would not. You are too soft-hearted! I still remember how you commended me for not shooting to kill on the one occasion when I have ever been accosted . . . of course, I realise there were special circumstances attaching to *that* particular case.'

Anne said nothing. Sir Tristram made one last attempt at pursuing the subject—'Had it been any common or garden ruffian that had attacked me, I daresay you might not have been quite so hot in his defence!'—but finding her still silent, eventually desisted, contenting himself with a final 'Well, I must not be jealous . . . I know all you ladies have a weakness for villains!' Anne smiled, but did not rise to the bait; and thereafter was left in peace for the remainder of the journey. Sir Tristram only sat back in his corner and looked at her sideways, which, however it might irritate, was at any rate to be preferred to conversation.

She had been dreading lest he take advantage of Miss Morcomb's inevitable invitation to "come inside" and "make himself at home"—"stay for just as long as he liked"—but either the prospect did not appeal or else he was on his best behaviour: he stayed only long enough to be polite, to take a glass of parsnip wine and pass favourable comment on the new furnishings for the schoolroom, and then, mercifully, was gone.

'What a very personable gentleman!' The parsnip wine, so early in the day, had flushed Miss Morcomb's cheeks an excitable pink. 'My dearest Anne! You must tell me if I speak out of turn, but . . . would it be premature in me to congratulate you?'

'As if that is not the outside of enough!' With fine disregard for the state of his wife's nerves, Jack slammed the drawing room doors hard behind him. Angrily, he strode across the room. 'It is finally and positively the last straw!'

'What is finally and positively the last straw?' Fanny, who had been idling away an empty half hour before dinner by re-arranging a bowl of pinks which stood upon a small table near the windows, spoke mildly, without even troubling herself to look up. 'What has happened to upset you?'

'What has happened to upset me? I will tell you what has happened to upset me! Richard is what has happened to upset me! I have just been approached by Porson. He informs me that Mr Wykeham has gone out and has very thoughtfully left a message for us . . . he has left a message with *Porson*. For *us*. He has not come to us and presented his excuses. Oh, no! He has left—'

'A message with Porson,' said Fanny. 'Quite. I think you have made your point. What is this message that he has left with Porson?'

'Oh! It is only to say that he has suddenly been called out and will not be with us for dinner . . . that he "might be back late" and that that being the case we need not trouble ourselves to wait up for him . . . that is all.' Jack flung himself down upon a chair: it creaked ominously beneath his weight. 'Nothing of any real consequence. Just another display of damned highhandedness and loutish ill manners. Just—'

'I hope everything is all right.' Fanny had stuck the last of the pinks back all anyhow into the bowl. 'I hope there is nothing wrong with Miss Fredericks.'

'Why should there be anything wrong with her?'

'She was taken very poorly—yesterday, when we were in Oxford. I thought it was merely Richard who had agitated her—'

'Richard is enough to agitate anyone!'

'Yes, yes, I am sure that he is! But were you not there, this morning, when that note came for him? Did you not observe the way, so soon as he had opened it and run his eye down the page, he instantly left the room? As if he wished to be by himself?'

'I cannot say that I did, but if I had I would have attached no significance to it. His reaction to every merest trifle is so extreme—'

'No! That is not fair! When one is in love, there is no such thing as a merest trifle. If Miss Fredericks is unwell, then he is bound to be concerned, and rightly so! I should think the less of him an he were not.'

'If Miss Fredericks is unwell, I see no reason why he should not have come to us and told us. He knows he would have all our sympathy.'

'Yes—' Fanny bit her lip. 'You are right. But in that case—'

'In that case he is simply behaving with his usual cavalier disregard of everyone else's comfort.' Jack snatched up his newspaper, and shook it open with an air of disgust. 'I am out of all charity with him.'

'You are always out of charity with him: that is nothing new.'

'Neither is his behaviour.'

'I disagree! It is not like Richard to go off without warning. He may turn *up* without warning; but once he is here, he is not as a rule inconsiderate.'

Behind his paper, Jack snorted.

'Wait!' Fanny suddenly pressed her fingers to her temples. 'There was another note came for him—about an hour ago. I remember Porson asking me if I knew where Mr Wykeham was to be found. I said I thought he might be in with you—'

'Well, he was not. I have scarcely seen him all day.'

'Neither have I,' said Fanny. 'Not since this morning. It is as if he has been deliberately hiding himself from us . . . Jack, I am going up to his room! I am going to see if there is anything there—any clue—any hint as to where he might have gone.'

'*I* am going to have my dinner,' said Jack. 'I no longer care where he has gone.'

Fanny looked at him, reproachfully.

'Just give me five minutes . . . that is all.'

'It had better be. I am not prepared to go hungry for him.'

Fanny was back almost immediately; well within the stipulated five minutes. Her normally cheeful countenance was puckered and distressed.

'Well?' said Jack. 'What have you discovered?'

'The worst . . . Miss Fredericks has cried off! I found the note beside his bed—I had taken in the contents before I realised what it was that I was reading . . . oh, Jack! How could she do so? I had not thought she could be so cruel! It only shows how deceived one may be in a person. I was prepared to swear that she was as much in love with him as he with her. And now this! Without so much as a word of explanation—just that she begs to be excused . . . small wonder if he has been hiding from us all day!'

Slowly, Jack laid down his newspaper.

'This is the very thing I had feared—the thing that I have feared all along . . . that at the last he would find himself let down. Dear God!' He passed a hand across his eyes. 'Is there never to be an end of it? For a short while one actually allowed oneself to hope—almost to *believe*—and now, in a moment, it is shattered! He will go back to his old ways—has probably already done so, if the truth were known. He is probably out there now, at this very moment—'

'Jack, for pity's sake! Do not say so!'

'Why not? Do you not like it? Then give me some other explanation for his absence!'

'I cannot, but I am certain there must be one. It is possible—' Fanny's face suddenly cleared—'it is possible he has gone over to Boswood to see Miss Fredericks and set things to rights between them . . . that is what it will be! The second note will have been from her, saying that the first was a mistake, or that it was—was written under duress, or—or some such thing . . . her brother, you know! He is obviously a tyrant. He will have forced her into it. And now she has arranged a secret meeting, and that is why Richard has gone off without telling us, because she has specifically requested him not to do so. I daresay he will be back within the hour, engaged to be married and informing us that the wedding is for next week!'

Jack shook his head.

'What a sad romancer you are . . . I do not wish to be shattering any illusions, but I am afraid it is far more likely that he is lurking somewhere in the shadows, with a scarf pulled over his face, preparing to play the same futile game that he has been playing for the past five years. It is only a question of time before someone puts a bullet through his brain. They damed nearly did so a day or two ago—I almost begin to think it is a pity they did not succeed, for I tell you plainly I cannot take much more of it!' He pushed back his chair. 'I am going to have my dinner. Do you intend joining me?'

Fanny heaved a sigh.

'I suppose there is not much else that one can do.'

'Not much else at all. I, for one, have dismissed it from my mind. I shall not think of it again. It is certainly not worth ruining a good dinner over.'

CHAPTER ELEVEN

If you would seek Revenge for a Past Injury, then you would do well to be in the vicinity of Hangman's Hill, on the Oxford-Abingdon Road, between the hours of seven-thirty and eight o'clock this night, when a maroon carriage drawn by two grey horses may prove of Interest to you. This intelligence is sent, not by a Well Wisher, but by one who makes no secret of having his Own Personal Axe to grind.

Richard's hand, in his coat pocket, closed over a sheet of paper already crumpled from repeated readings and re-readings. The cryptic message it contained gave no clue as to who the sender might be; but from the circumstance of having divulged to but the one person where he might currently be located, he was forced to the conclusion that it could have come only from Boswood, or from someone acquainted therewith. He suspected Sir Tristram—and suspecting Sir Tristram, could only suspect a trap. So be it. If trap there was, then he would fall into it. At least he would go down fighting; they would not get their hands on him without a struggle. Honour demanded that much. For the rest—

He shrugged. For the rest, he was past caring. If there were a gallows to hand, then let them use it. What, after all, did it matter? He had already lost everything that was worth losing. There was nothing more they could take from him—nothing, that is, of any value. He was not so strongly attached to the world as to place his own life in such category.

The mare, beneath him, shifted her weight and gave a small whinny of protest. He gentled her, leaning forward in the saddle to speak directly in her ear.

'Be patient, my beauty . . . if there is to be any action, it will be soon. We cannot now have long to wait.'

Anne's surprise at finding Adam come in the carriage to pick her up was exceeded only by her extreme relief at his not being Sir Tristram. Such misery had she been anticipating from a second journey spent in *his* company, it was not until they were under way that it occurred to her, there was every possibility of equal misery being endured from spending it in Adam's. If his intention were to lecture her yet again—

She risked a quick glance at him. He caught her eye before she was able to turn away; and instantly, as if it were a signal he had been waiting for, leaned towards her.

'Anne!'

He stretched out a hand: she shrank, involuntarily.

'Anne . . . forgive me!' There was a note of urgency in Adam's voice that she had not heard before. His body, quite suddenly, was shaking with violent tremors, his brow bathed in perspiration. 'Whatever has been done—whatever may be yet to come—it is not by my wishes! I am not a free agent! Sir Tristram—'

He broke off, groping for a handkerchief.

'Sir Tristram?' said Anne. She frowned. 'What has Sir Tristram to do with anything.'

'Only that—that it is he—'

'He?'

'Who has forced me! All these years . . . all these

years . . . and now—dear God!'

Anne regarded him, gravely.

'Are you trying to tell me that Sir Tristram has had some sort of hold over you? Are you saying that he . . . that he . . . *knew?*'

'Knew?' Adam thrust his handkerchief back in his sleeve. 'Knew what? What are you talking about?'

'You know what I am talking about! Adam . . . do not pretend! Not any more! Let us have the truth between us at last—let us be honest with one another! I know that you sent Richard away when he came to see me . . . I know that you did it, and I know why you did it. Until yesterday, I was in ignorance—I did not even suspect. Good God! How should I? My own brother! But then—then something—happened—which made me realise. It opened my eyes—made everything fall into place. All the things which had been so puzzling . . . but there is one thing that puzzles me still! Adam, why, in the first instance, did you choose to turn and run? Why did you not stay and—'

'And take my punishment?' Adam dropped his head into his hands. 'Because, I suppose, I am too much the coward . . . but, Anne, I have had my punishment! I have paid the price—over and over! Not just in money, though God knows Sir Tristram has lived well enough at my expense these past years . . . half the gaming tables in town have been financed with the cash he has screwed out of me.'

'He has actually been blackmailing you? But how? I don't understand!'

'He turned up at Boswood a few days after the—the incident—' Adam uttered the word with difficulty—'had occurred. By some devilish mischance, he happened to have been in the vicinity at the time.'

'You mean that he actually witnessed what happened?'

'From the start to the finish . . . oh! He was very civilised about it. He informed me that he was perfectly prepared to maintain his silence . . . for a price. And I have paid the price! I have paid it in misery, and in torment . . . in self-flagellation! If you knew how I have suffered . . . I have re-lived that day a thousand times! Not a waking moment but some part of it is with me. It haunts me both by day and night! What happened was the sheerest accident—the sheerest bad luck—and I have been harried and hounded as if it were a crime!'

'It can only be your own conscience that has made it seem so. At any moment you might have laid down your burden. Richard has always been there. You have always known where you might find him—or how to let him find you. Had you really wished, you might have expiated your guilt at any time by going to him and asking his forgiveness.'

'Ay! And having my head blasted off for my pains! He has had no right—no right!—to pursue me as he has! If anyone is to be held responsible for his sister's death, it is he!'

'If that is so, then you have been suffering needless torment all these years. You have allowed yourself to be blackmailed twice over—physically by Sir Tristram, and mentally by yourself. You have kept Isabella mewed up to no purpose, you have done your best to convince *me* that I am a useless invalid who must be confined for her own good—in short, you have destroyed her life and mine along with your own.'

'No—no!' Vehemently, Adam shook his head. 'Do not say that! Do not say it! Whatever has happened—whatever is still to come—the guilt is on his shoulders, not mine! He cannot be exonerated! By taking the law into his own hands, he has placed himself beyond its protection. I will not be held to blame! I will do what has to be done, and I—' He stopped. 'What is that? Did you hear something?' Feverishly, he plunged his hand into one of the side pockets of the carriage. 'Where are we? I cannot see! Are we—'

'At the place they call Hangman's Hill . . . Adam! Is this what you meant by saying you are not a free agent? Because if that is so, then it is simply not true! We are all of us free agents! You do not have to act as Sir Tristram tells you.'

'It is too late for that kind of talk . . . I am tired of living like a hunted animal.'

'Then the answer is in your own hands . . . *yours!* Not Sir Tristram's!'

'You are right,' said Adam. From the side pocket of the carriage he withdrew a pistol. 'It is in my own hands!'

'*Adam!*' Anne caught at his arm. 'For the love of God!'

'Leave me be!' Impatiently, he shook her off. 'The answer is in my own hands, and by the Lord I intend to—' He faltered. 'I intend to—'

'To what, my friend?'

'To—to take . . .' With a groan, Adam fell back. The pistol, unfired, slipped from his fingers. 'I cannot . . . cannot . . .'

'What is the problem, pray? Does your nerve fail you at the last minute?' The masked figure which appeared in the doorway had eyes for no one but Adam. 'Pick up your weapon, man, and play your part! I have waited five long years for this encounter . . . I will not be denied satisfaction now!'

'I cannot fight you.' Adam edged back into the corner of his seat. 'You must take your satisfaction as you can . . . it is not in me to kill a man.'

'No! You stop short of killing women!'

'It was an accident—an accident! I would not have had it happen for the world!'

'But nevertheless, it did happen—*did it not?* My sister died, and you got off scot free. Can you think of one good reason why I should not put a bullet through you?'

'None.' Adam's voice was the merest whisper. 'You must do what you want . . . I offer no resistance.'

'Damn you, man! What I want is for you to step outside and give me satisfaction!'

'Richard—' Anne spoke quietly, from out of the shadows. 'He has paid the price . . . do not torture him.'

'*Anne?*' The door of the carriage was flung open. 'What in the name of—'

'Be merciful! You said yourself, you were weary of this constant ache for revenge.'

'Ay! That was when I thought you were going to make a reformed character of me! What made you change your mind? The discovery that I was no better than—' he pulled the scarf from about his face—'than a common highwayman?'

'I never for one moment thought that you were a common highwayman!'

'Then why? *Why?* What made you write that note? But

twenty-four hours ago you were saying that you would marry me! What has happened in the interval? Is it something I have done? Something that I have said? Tell me!'

'Do you need to be told?' Adam spoke harshly. 'How could she marry you, knowing that her own brother was the one who had wronged you? For God's sake! Why do you not go ahead and put a bullet through me? By my own weakness I have caused so much distress to so many people that I almost begin to feel it is no more than I deserve.'

'It is Sir Tristram who deserves it,' said Anne.

'Sir Tristram! I would willingly put a bullet through *him.*'

'And not through me?' Adam hunched forward on his seat. 'Can we not bring an end to this charade? If you wish your revenge, then take it. I have told you . . . I will offer no resistance.'

'And I tell you, that that will not suit!'

'You insist that we play out the farce to its natural conclusion? Very well, then! Hand me my pistol: I will accommodate you.'

'Adam—Richard!' Anne caught imploringly at the latter's sleeve. 'I beg you . . . don't force him!'

'He is not forcing me,' said Adam. 'I am a free agent.'

'It is something that is necessary.' Gently, Richard prised open Anne's hand. 'A matter strictly between the two of us. A question of . . . honour.'

'Of self-respect,' said Adam. 'I take it you do not object to dispense with seconds?'

'Not in the least. I am perfectly willing to take your word that you will conduct yourself as a gentleman should.'

'And I yours.'

'So! What shall we say? Ten paces?'

'It sounds reasonable.'

'Reasonable? *Reasonable?* You step outside to kill each other and then you call it *reasonable?*'

'Anne . . . sweetheart!' Richard drew her to him. He bent, and dropped a light kiss on her forehead. 'Trust me,' he whispered.

Adam was already outside and waiting.

'I am ready,' he said, 'if you are.'

'I have been ready any time these past five years!' Richard

sprang lightly down on to the turf. 'Shall we mark the ground?'

'As you wish.'

'There is a patch over here would do for our purposes.'

They walked off together, shoulder to shoulder, in the gathering dusk. Francis, the coachman, peered round from his box to look at Anne.

'Would you wish me to be doing something, miss?'

'Such as what, would you suggest?' Anne spoke bitterly. 'Short of banging their heads together—'

'I have no objection to attempt it, miss, should you think it advisable.'

'That is heroic of you, Francis. Unfortunately, I do not think that either of them would thank you for it. Besides, I will not have you risk *your* neck only to save theirs. It is quite bad enough—'

She turned, abruptly, covering her ears with her hands. As she did so, two shots rang out. They were so close together as to be almost simultaneous. A tremor ran through her. To lose both brother and lover in one fell swoop—'

'There we are, then!' Richard's voice hailed her, cheerfully, from behind. 'All is over and you may open your eyes.'

She spun round.

'Where is Adam?'

'Prudently putting his coat back on, in case he should catch cold.'

'He is not hurt?'

'He is not hurt, and neither am I . . . to hurt each other was not the object of the exercise.'

Anne looked at him, thoughtfully.

'It was not?'

'Lord, no! What do you take us for, a couple of savages? We have done each other quite enough harm, over the years, without adding to it at the last.'

'I would agree with *that,*' said Anne. 'But if the intention was not to inflict mortal injury upon each other, may I ask what has been the purpose of it all?'

'Why, as I told you . . . it was a question of honour—or, in your brother's case, self-respect.'

'And honour has now been satisfied?'

'Completely.'

'And my brother's self-respect is restored?'

'That is something you will have to ask him, but as far as I am concerned there is no reason why it should not be.'

'I see.' Anne breathed, deeply. 'So what you are telling me is that two grown men may go out and settle a grievance which has rankled for five long years in as many seconds simply by firing pistols over each other's heads? If that is the case, I can only say it is a pity you did not get together a great deal sooner, for we might all of us have then been spared a vast amount of unnecessary suffering—and I believe I may speak for Fanny and Isabella in the matter, as well as for myself.'

'I am very sure that you may—and do not forget to add Jack to your list, while you are about it! He is one who would heartily endorse your sentiments. But there is just one flaw in your argument.'

'Oh? And what is that?'

'Simply that if your brother and I had got together sooner, the chances are we should have blasted each other's heads off in good earnest . . . come, now!' He pulled her towards him. 'Tell me that I am forgiven, and say that you will marry me.'

'I will certainly marry you—I am not at all sure that you are forgiven. You have caused me a very nasty fright, and all, apparently, to no purpose. If you had *intended* to fire over each other's heads, why could you not have said so at the outset?'

'Because honour would not then have been satisfied, nor self-respect restored!'

There was a pause; then: 'Of course not,' said Anne. 'How silly of me! I wonder I should not have seen it for myself . . .'

'I assure you,' said Jack, 'it gives me no pleasure to be proved right.'

'That is just as well,' said Fanny, 'since you have not yet been proved so.'

'No?' Jack took out his watch and made a business of consulting it. 'It now wants but three minutes to eleven o'clock. When those three minutes are up, I intend to instruct Porson to bolt the doors and to retire to my bed. You, of course, must do as you see fit. If you wish to sit up half the night worrying yourself sick whilst he rampages about the countryside, then that is your concern. I shall not attempt to interfere. For my part—'

'For your part, you have already said . . . you intend telling Porson to bolt the doors and then retiring to your bed, and I am not at all sure but while we have been talking—' Fanny broke off a moment, and listened. 'Yes!' She sprang up, out of her chair. 'That is Richard—I recognise his voice!'

The doors were thrown open. Richard, somewhat dust-caked and dishevelled, surveyed his hosts with an air of mild surprise.

'What! You are still up? I thought I told you not to wait?'

'I suppose—' Jack spoke drily—'that one may do as one chooses in one's own house?'

'Oh! By all means. It is just that I did not wish to inconvenience you.'

'Your thoughtfulness astonishes.'

'Well, but that is why I left that note with Porson. I knew you would be worried, if I did not.'

'Worried?' said Jack. 'What makes you think that I should be worried?'

'Oh, not you! I know that you have long since given me up as a bad job. I was referring to Fanny, rather than you. It is Fanny who cares for me—it is Fanny who still has faith in me. It is Fanny, therefore, to whom I shall give my news.'

'If you are going to tell us that you have been up to your old tricks and have had another bullet put in you,' said Jack, 'then she is welcome to it.'

'Up to my old tricks?' Richard regarded him, haughtily. 'And what, pray, gave you that notion?'

'Oh, he has been on about it all evening! He has been trying to make believe that you had gone out on purpose to hold people up. Take no notice of him, he is nothing but a misery . . . as if you would do such a thing!'

'As if I would!'

'The very idea is preposterous. After all—' Fanny looked at him, anxiously—'if Miss Fredericks is to marry you—'

'She is,' said Richard. 'That is what my news is . . . she has forgiven me all my sins and is going to make a reformed character of me. And we are not going to lose any time about it, either! I am deputed to apply for a special licence, and to inform you that the marriage is to take place next week.'

'There!' said Fanny. She nodded triumphantly at Jack. 'What did I tell you? I have been right all along . . .'

GUARDIAN OF THE HEART
by Caroline Courtney

The Marquis of Rossington was a libertine. The ladies of the London ton and the Versailles court loved him far too well for their own good and learned too late that he loved no one. To this handsome, bitter man, Sir John Lawley had, by mistake, assigned the guardianship of his beautiful young daughter. No man, save the Marquis, could look upon her silvery blonde innocence and deliberately plan her undoing. Any man, save the Marquis, would have seen that he, as much as she, would soon need a guardian of the heart. . . .

SBN: 0 552 11605 X Price: 95p